THE GIRL
WHO FELL
TO EARTH

PATRICIA FORDE

Little
Island
Books create waves

THE GIRL WHO FELL TO EARTH

First published in 2023 by
Little Island Books
7 Kenilworth Park
Dublin 6w
Ireland

A British Library Cataloguing in Publication record for
this book is available from the British Library.

Cover illustration by Jeff Langevin
Typeset by Tetragon, London
Printed in Poland by L&C

Print ISBN: 978-1-915071-43-9
Ebook ISBN: 978-1-915071-45-3

Little Island has received funding to support this book from
the Arts Council of Ireland / An Chomhairle Ealaíon

The author acknowledges her receipt of an English Literature Bursary from
The Arts Council of Ireland/An Comhairle Ealaíon for the writing of this novel

10 9 8 7 6 5 4 3 2 1

For my husband, Padraic

HOW IT STARTED

I remember the day it started. I was in class, supposedly listening to Dr Jake Watson talking about DNA. DNA was Dr Watson's passion, if you could imagine a large slow-moving sloth having a passion. The doc had been droning on at us for over an hour when, finally, we were allowed to go to our individual celloscope stations. This was the highlight of his lecture, where we got to spit on a tiny glass slide and see our own DNA. Wow! How lucky could we get? Doc Watson made it sound like we'd won a prize. What was it with scientists that they thought everything was so fascinating? But I'd promised Dad that I'd do my best with this module and so I made a big effort to listen.

'You will all please now look at your DNA structure. You will see that it looks like a honeycomb, with the hexagonal shape we associate with our DNA.'

I looked, but I had no idea what he was talking about. My DNA didn't look anything like a hexagon. I adjusted the eye-piece and tried again – still no hexagon. I was about to put my hand up when something stopped me. All the other students were looking through their lenses and nodding.

'Pick up your tablets,' Dr Watson said, 'and draw what you see.'

Dava, the ultra-clever science nerd to my right, had already begun to draw. Peering over her shoulder, I saw a series of hexagons.

I grabbed the celloscope and glared through the lens again. My DNA looked like a twisty rope ladder. I looked across the room to where Rio was sitting, hoping to catch her eye, but she was talking to the boy beside her, her head bent, her hands gesticulating wildly, as they always did when she was excited about something, and she didn't notice.

Maybe the slide was the wrong way around? I repositioned it and looked again. There was no doubt now. My DNA looked nothing like the other students' DNA.

I stepped back from the celloscope as though it had bitten me. A cold feeling ripped through my body. I felt like I was free-falling into a deep hole.

Then the real question came, the words tumbling one over the other, like waves racing for shore.

How could that be?

1

knew who I was, I told myself. My biological father was Lucas Evan. My biological mother was Della Gular. Thus my surname – Evangular. Evan and Gular. I was a Terrosian, a citizen of the best planet in the universe, the planet of Terros. I had been grown in an artificial womb in the Blue Lab like all my friends and was delivered full term at twelve months.

My mother said that I was a cute baby, but she could be a bit biased. She is something of a beauty herself, and all my friends say that Dad is nothing if not handsome, which, though nausea-inducing, is possibly true. Mum and Dad had come to look at me once a month in the Blue Lab, watching me grow from a blob (albeit a *cute* blob) into a strapping baby of three point three kilograms at full term.

I also knew that I didn't have some terrible disease, because I had a full medical every month, whether I liked it or not, just like every other teenager on Terros. I had experienced the odd glitch – to be honest, more than the odd glitch; I had once thrown a fever in the middle of the night that had terrified my parents – I had some minor allergies and the occasional headache. Seb Roy, my medical supervisor, had always taken care of me and assured me that these were things that I would eventually grow out of.

But none of my friends had experienced glitches. It was one of the few things that I didn't or couldn't discuss with my parents. It made them too anxious.

When I was younger, my mother had warned me never to discuss these glitches with anyone other than Seb Roy, and I had done exactly as she told me. Seb Roy had convinced me that there was nothing to worry about, and over the years I had allowed myself to believe that.

So why wasn't my brain happy to accept that now? Why was it nibbling away at me in the dark of the night and keeping me awake?

I had to find out why my DNA didn't look like anyone else's DNA. Obviously, I had done something wrong in Doc Watson's class and had messed up the test. It wouldn't be the first time. Even my best friends would say that I wasn't exactly a natural at science. Still, I had to know the truth; and that meant going back to the lab to have the Evaluator analyse my DNA properly. I could have asked Doc Watson about it, but something told me not to draw attention to the situation until I had an answer. If there was something weird about me, I wanted to be the first to know about it.

It would be a challenge to get into the lab without being discovered, but that wasn't what worried me. What would the Evaluator say? That was what really bothered me. I'd been to enough biology sessions to know that the Evaluator contained the most advanced science available on Terros. Every atom of knowledge, every new discovery, every proven theory was uploaded to the Evaluator. It also contained all our personal information, our medical history, our family history. It was one of our greatest inventions and I knew it had the answers that I wanted – as long as I didn't get caught before I could ask the question.

I chose a quiet mid-week night for my expedition. I couldn't risk going there during the day when the place was awash with students and scientists, not to mention security. At night, there were no students and only a skeleton crew of guards. There were always random scientists there, but I would have to risk that.

8

The laboratory was a short walk from our house, and I hoped I could be there and back within an hour. Mum and Dad were relaxing together, chatting in the family pod, laughing at some story Dad was telling about an experiment that had gone wrong.

I stood at the door watching them for a second, wishing I could go back to the way things had been before I knew anything about my strange DNA.

'What's happening, Aria?' Mum said when she saw me standing there. She was wearing a wine-coloured bodysuit with silver fastenings, and her curly black hair flowed down her back, freed from the tight bun she normally wore to work.

'I thought I might power down,' I said. 'It's been a long day.'

'I bet.' Dad grinned. 'All that gossiping with the girls and –'

Mum gave him a friendly punch. 'Respect!' she said in a mock cross voice. 'We women do not gossip!'

'Good night, baby girl,' Dad said, and for once I didn't protest about being called a baby.

I left the room and headed to my sleep pod. I knew that they wouldn't disturb me until morning. They never did. They trusted me. That thought didn't sit well with me. I hated lying to them, but it had to be done.

An hour later, I slipped through the back door and out into the night. I hurried across the darkening park, keeping to the shadows.

Ahead of me, the twin towers of The Hub pulsed orange and blue, their gleaming curves twisting brazenly, as they reached high into the night sky. This was the heart of our community, the seat of power and the place where we came to be educated. There was nothing more important than education on our planet.

I felt a surge of pride, the way I always did, when I saw the towers. They were a symbol for all the brilliant things the people of my planet had done and would do in the future. We were the most advanced people to *ever* evolve, and I was so proud to be part of it all.

I hurried on, getting more and more nervous as I got nearer. The gauge on my bodysuit glowed fluorescent. My blood pressure was on the rise, my pulse galloping.

Taking a deep breath, I walked briskly up to the front door of The Hub. I raised my hand to the electronic eye, hoping that my student identity would get me in, even though I was never supposed to be there in the middle of the night.

The eye blinked. The screen lit up.

SECURITY QUESTION:
HAVE YOU A LEGITIMATE REASON TO BE HERE?

It seemed like an innocent question and not an awfully scientific one, but I knew how this worked. The eye was a lie detector, a sneaky device that could read the activity in my brain through the chip embedded over my left eye. But I had been raised in a world run by scientists. I knew that a lie was only a lie if you believed it to be so.

I looked at the eye.

'Yes,' I said.

I needed to know who I really was. That was a legitimate reason, wasn't it?

I had to believe this. If I didn't, I was about to witness an explosion of flashing lights, accompanied by deafening sirens and some very unfriendly security staff.

My heart beat painfully in the silence. The eye blinked again. The door slid open.

I was in.

I hurried down the dark corridors. Through the translucent doors, I could see that the White Laboratory was deserted. I pushed

10

the door gently and it slid open with a soft whisper. The long room was eerily quiet and lit by a soft tawny light. Rows of desks and chairs stood like sentries in the half-light, and beyond them I could see the Evaluator at the top of the room. It was egg-shaped, its skin made from a single sheet of rantam, satin-smooth and silver grey.

The screen lit up as I approached it. I could see it scanning my retina, establishing that I was a student.

PLEASE CHOOSE YOUR AREA OF INTEREST.

A list appeared. I chose biology, and that threw up another menu.

CELLULAR ANALYSIS
TISSUE ANALYSIS
DNA ANALYSIS

I touched the last option and waited. The screen transformed.

EXHALE ONTO SCREEN IN 3 ... 2 ... 1 ...

I blew. My breath misted the pristine glass.

The Evaluator's screen shuddered and letters began to form.

H ...

And then I heard footsteps. My heart lurched. I looked around desperately. I had to find somewhere to hide.

There was a storage area under the main utility bench, and I just managed to squeeze inside, my knees pressed up against my mouth and my arms wrapped around my body. I swiped the air with my hand and the door of the storage space glided silently across two-thirds of the way and then stopped. I suspected that my bulk was blocking the visual field, but before I could do anything about it the laboratory door opened. The feet stopped right in front of me. Two men. If they looked down they would see me.

I tried not to move, not to breathe.

'Have you decided to put yourself forward?' a voice I didn't recognise said. 'You would win easily. Your work is ambitious and your record unblemished.'

'Yes,' a second man answered in a clipped tight voice. 'I told parliament today that I would like to be considered in the leadership contest.'

I knew that voice. Seb Roy, my medical supervisor and one of our top scientists, also a good friend of my parents. I could see him in my mind's eye, with his floppy dark hair that fell over his right eye and his slightly crooked mouth.

'I would be honoured to run your campaign. We will have to persuade people that you are the only man for the job. They need to get to know you better. We need to get you out there …'

'I'm looking forward to it,' Seb said.

'There will be a thorough investigation into every aspect of your life,' the second man said. 'But as I said, you have an unblemished record.'

Thoughts buzzed like bees in my brain. Seb wanted to be the next leader of Terros?

'Indeed,' Seb snapped, and I heard the sharp tip-tap of feet leaving the room.

At that exact moment, the Evaluator pinged as it refreshed the page. I edged the door of the storage space ever so slightly away from me. Through the opening I watched in horror as Seb Roy walked over to the now glowing screen, his long legs eating up the distance.

No! A voice was screaming in my head. *Don't look at the screen.*
'Seb!'

He took a step backwards and glanced around. The other man was calling from the corridor outside.

I held my breath. Seb's eyes seemed to be looking straight at me. He hesitated for another moment, then turned sharply and walked away. I waited. I didn't care how long I had to wait. I'd come for answers and I wasn't leaving without them. After ten slow and painful minutes, I thought I might risk opening the door fully. I peered into the vast room and saw the high desks loom out of the dusk, standing on one leg like storks. I tumbled out and made straight for the Evaluator. The screen had gone to sleep again so I touched the cool glass interface. Immediately a series of letters appeared.

HUMAN/DOMINANT/MATERNAL

2

The days that followed were a bit of a blur. I couldn't stop thinking about the twisting rope ladders and the words on the screen, and I couldn't talk to anyone. The shock was like ice water trickling through me. I needed time to work things out, to think of a plan. As soon as I opened my mouth about my DNA, my world, as I knew it, would be over and I wasn't about to let that happen.

Terros was for Terrosians and no-one else. Nobody was allowed on Terros unless they were born here. That was how we protected our immune systems. We Terrosians didn't die unless by accident. There was no way we could risk all of that by allowing people in from other planets who didn't have our strength and could bring in all kinds of disease. It was one of the few unnegotiable rules on our planet. We went out into the universe but others did not come to us.

I was also trying to deal with the crushing disappointment of knowing that I wasn't actually a Terrosian. I was from the Shadow Planet, a place that was little more than a giant laboratory with no history, no achievements – an embarrassment of a planet. That was where humans lived. We'd learnt all about them last year.

To make matters worse, it was Terros Commemoration Week, when our entire planet came together to celebrate Terros and the revolution of one thousand years ago. This year, the celebration took place on a Tuesday. That evening, when I came home from school, my parents were all ready.

'We should get down early, Aria,' my mother said when I walked in. 'I want to have time to chat to people. It's been so busy lately, I've hardly seen anyone.'

She was dressed from head to toe in gold. The light bounced off her suit and highlighted the copper undertones of her dark skin. Her long black hair was braided and beaded with tiny jewels. I don't think I'd ever seen her look more beautiful.

'Go and change quickly!' she said. 'I've left something in your room.'

I went down to my pod and opened the door. On the bed was a beautiful new bodysuit – indigo blue with a sharp green trim. It was stunning. We rarely dressed up in our house, so it was always exciting to get a new, special suit. Only I didn't feel excited. My heart felt like a lump of lead. I put the suit on and, as I was making my way back to Mum, Dad appeared. He looked up at me and I saw his sharp eyes soften.

'You look wonderful, Aria,' he said. 'Blue is your colour.'

He grinned, his teeth white against his sandy-coloured skin.

'Come on!' Mum shouted from outside. 'We're going to be late!'

We walked to Terros Square, the central meeting point for our entire planet, where all major ceremonies took place and were beamed all across our world. We went along with everyone else, and drank hot chocolate and ate the small crisp rose-scented biscuits that were all part of the tradition. I just wanted to cry. It should have been the perfect night; the three moons circling one another in a clear, bright sky and a gentle breeze rippling the surface of the lake. Even though it was spring, and the seeds of the next harvest had been planted, the government had allowed us to have three days with no rain to celebrate our planet's holiday.

On previous anniversaries, I had been up at the top of the square with Rio and a gang of our friends, jumping and cheering, full of pride, but not tonight. I had told Rio and another friend, Karla, that I had to stay with my parents and, though Rio gave me a funny look, they accepted my lie without questioning me. I didn't think I could manage to fake the excitement I normally felt at being a Terrosian and I knew that Rio would notice. She knew me better than anyone else.

That night in the square, we watched the Icarus Wall, a giant screen that told the story of the great floods and natural disasters of over a thousand years ago that had led scientists to take over the world. Since then, the planet had completely healed and the leaders had made huge advances in knowledge. The disasters of the past were rapidly disappearing into the mists of time. For Terros, the future was bright.

When the screen disappeared, the sky lit up with enormous light-carved creatures that soared over the crowd, ducking and diving, almost touching the hands upstretched to them. The colours bled on to the gathering, streams of vivid blue and electric orange, and then re-formed and re-shaped into birds of every hue and type. They were dazzling, saturated in colour, with feathers that looked as if you could stroke them and long metallic claws that glinted in the light of the moons.

The crowd gasped, their voices following the birds up into the night sky. And then, with a blinding flash of gold, the entire square and surrounding streets transformed into a never-ending ocean with waves rippling and silver fish jumping triumphantly. Before we could fully take in what was happening, the scene changed again and we were surrounded by snowy mountains and a purple sky peppered with silver stars.

The illusions were incredible and the people in the square drank them up, but I couldn't enjoy the spectacle. My worries were still eating away at me. I looked up at my parents. They were holding hands and my father had his other arm around my shoulder. I could feel the warmth of his fingers through my bodysuit. I looked up at him and at Mum, and a painful thought floated to the surface of my mind. Were they even my parents? They had to be, I told myself, but how did that sit with my funny DNA? Was my mother also a creature of the Shadow Planet, a human? These were the sorts of questions that had been tormenting me, and I had no answer to any of them.

When the illusions drew to an end, everyone cheered and hugged one another and shouted 'Terros! Terros!' at the tops of their voices. Then came the roll-call of honour, where parliament called out the names of citizens of Terros who had advanced the cause of our planet in the last twelve months. You could almost touch the pride that we had in our world, this extraordinary place that we had created.

Rio and I dreamt of being on the roll-call one year, though we both knew that was far more likely to happen to Rio than to me. Still, I could dream, couldn't I? I wanted to be someone special, someone that would be remembered for helping push Terros forward.

Rio was totally passionate. I always envied her that. She was a scientist. It was in her genes and in every cell of her body. She never had to work at it.

I, on the other hand, wasn't passionate about science, and I wasn't that good at it. My father was a scientist, a marine biologist, and a good one too, though not as highly regarded as Seb and the others on the top layer. My mother was a teacher, a nurturer of talent. She worked with children who had exceptionally high IQs. I wasn't like her either. I wasn't as kind or as patient.

I loved words. I loved painting pictures with them, choosing them carefully, getting a feel for them before passing them on to a reader. Writing was a hobby, though, not a way of life on Terros, so my interest in writing wasn't encouraged. My readers were my family and friends, and some of those only read my stories to please me. On Terros, we already had all the literature we would ever need – all the literature, all the art, all the music. We didn't need new stuff. Parliament said there was no need to waste resources producing more.

I had been genetically designed to be a scientist. Certain genes had been tweaked when I was developing in the Blue Laboratory, and even though it wasn't absolutely guaranteed, the odds were good that I would like science and be good at it. I did admire people who were good at science with all my heart. I loved everything that they had achieved. But I had no feeling for it, no talent. My parents had reassured me. It takes time, they'd said. For some people, they have to be fully grown before their innate talents kick in.

Next year, I would turn fifteen, and I could see that my parents' attitude was changing. I often caught them exchanging anxious looks when they saw my school scores, and Dad had taken to giving me a bit of coaching after school. It hadn't helped. My scores were still average at best. I could download all the information in the world to my hippocampus, and I did, but I couldn't analyse it or be creative with it. I loved listening to Rio, though. When she talked, her green eyes flashed, alive with enthusiasm. She was always so excited about new discoveries and new ideas, but the day before the celebrations, I had interrupted her.

'Rio,' I said, 'we don't have the same DNA as people on any other planet, do we?'

She looked at me quizzically, her eyes wide, her head slightly tilted to one side.

'The same DNA? Of course not, Aria. Why would we have? We don't even have the same DNA that *we* had one thousand years ago. Once we discovered that we could take apart the building blocks and put them back together in a different pattern, then anything was possible. We changed our DNA and we'll probably change it again at some point. Have any of you seen the paper that Dora Lebons wrote recently? It's fascinating.'

And she was off again, but I wasn't listening. I was from another planet – or at least I had DNA from another planet. What would Rio and my friends think if they knew that? It didn't matter what way I looked at it, I couldn't understand how that could have happened. Nobody was allowed on Terros unless they were born here. So how had I got here? And how had no-one discovered my human DNA before? It made no sense.

The crowd in the square began to move off, their voices carrying on the night air. Mum and Dad were chatting with a woman dressed in a fire-red bodysuit and carrying a balloon hologram on a string. I was so distracted, I hardly noticed when Rio appeared beside me.

'What's up, Aria?' she said. Her close-cropped hair framed her elfin face, and her eyebrows were drawn together in a frown. 'You're in strange humour lately. I don't think I've ever seen you so serious. What's going on?'

'Nothing,' I said. 'I can be serious, you know. I'm not a total air-head.'

My tone was sharper than I meant it to be, and I saw her flinch.

'I never said you were an air-head.' She didn't say much more, but I knew I'd hurt her.

'Sorry,' I said. 'I didn't mean it to come out like that.'

Rio looked at me and I could see the concern in her eyes. 'You OK, my friend?'

She reached out and touched my hand and I wanted to tell her everything like I always did. There was no-one smarter than Rio or as kind, but I couldn't discuss this with her – at least not till I had an explanation. Finding out who I was, that was something I would have to do on my own.

'I'm fine,' I said. 'I really have to get home now, though. I'll see you tomorrow.'

I walked away as quickly as I could, afraid to look back. I knew Rio would be watching me, her head to one side, her huge brain trying to figure out what was happening.

I didn't have time to think about that now. I was due to make my first journey away from Terros in a few weeks. Every year, students were paired with senior scientists and made their first trip away from the home planet. Putting young people with highly experienced people was one of the ways we passed knowledge from one generation to the next. For months, everyone at school had been talking about little else, but I really wasn't that interested. I hadn't cared where they sent me or who I went with, but now, that had all changed. Now, I didn't care where I went to as long as it wasn't to the Shadow Planet. I couldn't face going there and seeing what I had come from. I can't explain it but I knew I couldn't face it. I couldn't think about anything else apart from the fact that I didn't belong on Terros any more.

Even thinking about it made me feel sick with loneliness. All the things I had taken for granted were no more: my citizenship, my place in my family, all of it. I felt like the ground beneath me had given way and I was looking up at the world from a deep, dark hole.

I knew already that Dad was going to the Shadow Planet. I'd overheard him talking to Mum about it, but he would never have told me.

A student's first trip was an important one, a coming-of-age, a milestone. The student and their mentor were for ever bound by that, and the relationship was special. Part of the excitement around the first trip was that the details were top secret. No-one knew who their mentor would be or to where they would be sent.

Dad was going to the Shadow Planet but none of my friends wanted to go there. No-one ever wanted to go there. People wanted to go to exciting planets, places we still knew little about. The Shadow Planet – a big laboratory which had been examined and analysed for years – was about as exciting as last night's dinner. The previous year, a really bright student had gone and absolutely hated it. He had asked to be brought home early and everyone said that it had damaged his life prospects.

I hoped I was headed for some planet way off in the opposite direction, preferably one inhabited by exotic birds and with fabulous food, but there was nothing I could do to control things. Like everyone else, I had to wait and see.

3

I didn't want to go to the Shadow Planet but I did want to find out more about it. I started to research it and the people who lived there, finding out everything that I could. It was the biggest experiment we had ever undertaken on our planet. We'd found an empty planet in a far off-galaxy that could sustain life and we'd taken it over. We'd seeded it with the DNA needed to develop human life and then speeded up their evolution. They looked like us because their DNA was based on our DNA. For the last one thousand years, we'd watched from afar as they had grown and developed, fought wars, cured disease and made music. They were *us* a thousand years ago, before we learnt that even our DNA could be changed to our advantage. And they had no idea what was going on. They didn't know that they were our laboratory, that they only existed to serve us, or that we watched them all the time.

My parents were surprised at my sudden interest in science and then delighted. The whole thing made me feel terrible. I hadn't realised how much it would mean to them if I suddenly became the girl I was meant to be. For years, I had fooled myself, thinking that they didn't mind and that they'd be happy whatever I chose to do with my life. Now, I could see that they desperately wanted me to be a scientist.

On Announcement Day, we were all nervous. I sat at the high table with the other fourteen-year-olds waiting for the big reveal.

22

Rio was sitting on the bench opposite me and I could almost feel her excitement. She was hoping to be sent to one of the planets in the Orange Tide, a constellation far from here, with creatures who looked nothing like us and didn't use any known language to communicate. I caught her eye and smiled over at her. She gave me a teeny-weeny wave and looked away. Things had become a bit strained between us since we'd had a discussion about the Shadow Planet. Rio had noticed me doing research and couldn't understand why I'd suddenly taken an interest in it.

'I'm curious, that's all,' I'd said. 'I'd like to see what we were like before the revolution and that's what the Shadow Planet is – us a thousand years ago.'

I had decided to confide in her. Rio was my friend and she would help me like I'd help her if the tables were turned. I opened my mouth to tell her but Rio was talking.

'Totally feral!' Rio had scoffed. 'That's what we were like and that's what they are like. The place is a mess and its inhabitants are filthy, full of disease and entirely out of control. Do you know how many new people they have there every year?'

I shook my head.

'Eighty-three million! Can you imagine?'

I couldn't. We were only allowed one child per couple and some people didn't even bother with that. How could the Shadow Planet support that many people?

'They've polluted the place and have produced a greenhouse effect which is warming up the planet to a dangerous level. So they're stupid as well as dirty. Actually, I don't think we were *ever* that bad, even a thousand years ago. And you know that there is no intervention before birth and that some of them are born with all kinds of problems?'

I nodded. I knew that there were lots of people with malfunctions on the Shadow Planet. Some people couldn't see, some were deaf, some couldn't walk. The Shadow Planet was an experiment. Our people had designed it to see what happens to living beings when there is almost no interference from science. Its people had been grown in our laboratories, engineered to speed up evolution and then transplanted to the Shadow Planet. The humans had never managed to adjust their DNA, as we had. They still had the DNA that we gave them a thousand years ago. It sounds awful, but apparently we learn loads about ourselves just by studying the things that can go wrong.

'I know we need them,' Rio said. 'The scientist in me knows that we can learn a lot from studying them, but I'd hate to have to go there. I really find the people who live there disgusting.'

She shuddered as she said it and I wanted to slap her. I knew she was only telling me the truth, but it felt like a kick in the stomach. I tried to imagine her being supportive and comforting me when I told her the truth about my own DNA, but my powers of fantasy didn't stretch that far. I knew she'd be disgusted.

Seb Roy and Mella Dime appeared on the dais at the top of the room. They were in charge of all mission assignments for the young people in our district. Mella was tall and stately with a long plait of blue-black hair and skin that glowed. She carried herself like an old-fashioned ship in full sail, the picture of elegance. Beside her, tall Seb Roy seemed short and maybe even a little awkward. I narrowed my eyes. This was it. Mella Dime was talking in her raspy, singsong voice: '... and so I will now read out your missions and mentors. Please listen carefully.'

I crossed my fingers. Mella droned on and on until finally I heard my own name.

'Aria Evangular.'

Mella paused and looked up until she caught my eye. Every fibre of my being pulsed with anticipation.

'The Shadow Planet. Your mentor is Lucas Evan.'

Something exploded in my brain. Was I imagining things? The Shadow Planet! I couldn't quite take it in. I saw Dad put his head down. How had this happened? Young people were never paired with a parent as a mentor. All around me my friends threw me sympathetic looks, and Rio looked like someone had just slapped her. I saw Dad lean over and say something to Mella, who looked at the screen in front of her and nodded. Seconds later, Mella confirmed that Rio was headed for the Orange Tide, but I barely took that in. Mella's words seemed to hang in the air – 'the Shadow Planet'. And I was going with Dad.

When it was over, Dad approached me with a concerned look on his face.

'Sorry about that, Ari,' he said. 'You weren't supposed to be the one travelling with me. The truth is we've been given a very special mission. I can't say any more at the moment but I need you to be mature about this. It's important for all of us.'

No! I wanted to scream but I made myself stay calm.

'Can't we ask for it to be changed?' I said. 'It isn't where I want to go.'

Dad shook his head.

'I'm sorry, Ari. The decision is final. But we'll be together and you're coming at a really good time. Go home now and I will explain everything when we are on our own.'

I had no idea what was going on, but I did what I was told. I went home and waited.

Much later, at home in our own house, Dad told me what he knew.

'This is a top-secret mission, Aria. We can't discuss it with anyone. We're starting all over again with the Shadow Planet – a new beginning,' he said, his face unusually stern. 'We have no further need for its people. They have created a scenario where that planet can no longer support them. There's no point in moving them to somewhere else – we know that their behaviour won't change. We are going to wipe them out, quickly and humanely. Better that than a slow lingering death with famine and floods. And have no doubt, Aria, that is what lies ahead for them. They've reached the tipping point. The planet will soon be too hot to support human life. There is no going back.'

He paused, his eyebrows drawn together in a frown.

'Seb is putting all his trust in us,' he said then. 'You are very honoured to be allowed to be part of this. You will be remembered, Aria, when the history of Terros is written.'

His words rushed towards me. I tried to take them in. I was going on a top-secret mission. I was going to be remembered as someone who played a role in our history. This was all I had dreamt of – except I was going to the Shadow Planet and not to some exotic, unexplored planet.

I made myself focus on what Dad was saying.

'We're going to release a virus. Two doses. The first will soften up the immune system, though the majority of humans won't have any symptoms at that stage. The second dose will eradicate all human life. You and I will deliver the first dose at a specific location. Other teams will deal with other locations across the globe. The second dose will be administered later.'

Dad's words were playing in my head but I couldn't quite process them. *The second dose will eradicate all human life.* That's what he'd said.

Dad must have seen that there was something troubling me.

'Don't worry,' he said, with a reassuring smile. 'I know it's a lot to take in, but I will brief you fully before we leave. And remember they don't feel things the way we do. We are saving them from themselves and giving them a peaceful way to die.'

I was still reeling from the shock as he walked away. I had the same DNA as the people who lived on the Shadow Planet – and I would be on the Shadow Planet when the first dose was released. Would it kill me? I tried to fight the wave of panic building inside me. I was young and strong with an almost perfect immune system. I would be fine. I had to be.

The following weeks passed in a mad whirl of hustle and bustle. There were the daily briefings from my father, the medical tests with Seb Roy and my mother fussing about clothes and other practical things that I might need. The sessions with Seb were tense, to say the least. He didn't say much, he just checked my inoculations and my iron levels, gave me more vitamins and advised me that on the Shadow Planet my skin would be exposed to stronger sunlight than at home, though at this time of year, that wouldn't matter so much. I watched him carefully during our sessions together. Had he noticed my strange DNA? If he had, why hadn't he said anything? More than once I opened my mouth to ask him and then just as quickly closed it again.

I thought about nothing other than the mission. We were only delivering the first dose. By the time the second dose was released, I would be safely home on Terros. I had to believe that. I had to. But it didn't stop the feeling of dread that had settled in my stomach or ease the throbbing pain over my eyes every time my mind went there.

I hardly saw Rio or any of my friends. Like me, they were busy getting ready for their first missions. And then, the night before we were due to travel, I ran into Rio on my way home from Seb's clinic. We chatted for a few minutes about our missions; though, to be honest, we talked mostly about Rio's mission. I avoided talk of the Shadow Planet, in case I gave anything away. But I could see the pity in her eyes.

'Be careful,' I said to her as we got ready to say goodbye. 'Don't take any risks.'

She smiled. 'I won't. What is your mission anyway?' she said lightly.

I remembered what Dad had told me to say. 'We are going to collect data about the effects of air pollution on sea life.'

She nodded. 'I'm sorry Aria,' she said. 'I'm sure your next mission will be far more exciting.'

I didn't answer. Instead, I looped my little finger around her little finger.

'Friends for ever,' I said, doing what we used to do when we were five years old.

Rio burst out laughing. 'Friends for ever,' she agreed, and suddenly all the tension between us evaporated. Rio put her arms around me and we hugged.

'You'll do great,' she said. 'Because you are great.'

'And when I get home,' I said, 'you'll tell me how you conquered a distant planet and learnt everything we'll ever need to know to live happily ever after.'

'But of course,' Rio said with a grin.

I turned to leave.

'Aria!' she said.

I stopped.

'Come home safely. This is where you belong.'

Her words felt better than any hug. *This is where you belong*. That was all I wanted in that second. I wanted so badly to belong. My eyes flushed with hot tears but for once I couldn't find any words. I just stood there and watched her go.

4

The following day, as I hurtled through space, Rio's words rang in my ears. The morning had been a fog of last-minute instructions and goodbyes. Mum had come with us to the launch centre and I'd hugged her for a second or two longer than was strictly necessary. I felt a lump forming in my throat as she stroked my hair like she used to do when I was a small girl. I wanted to tell her everything, to pour out my worries like water from a jug, but I knew I couldn't. My mother could do a lot of things but I knew she couldn't change my DNA.

Minutes later we were in the *Veres*, my dad's ship, ready to go. I took a final look at my home planet, trying to drink in every detail, then buckled my restrainer. Dad glanced across at me and smiled. Within seconds we were launching.

I clenched my eyes and tried to concentrate on my breathing. I tried not to think about the fact that we were travelling ten thousand times faster than the speed of light. I looked at Dad for reassurance, but he was busy inputting data. Twenty minutes into the voyage, we separated from the launcher. I could imagine the trail of blue stars stretching out behind the *Veres*. Tiny pulsating stars, the only sign of the dark energy that allowed us to travel at warp speed and leave no pollutant behind us.

My heart slowed. I opened my restrainer. It felt good. Weightless, I floated away from my seat, bouncing my head off the cushioned ceiling.

'Adjust your oxygen levels, Ari,' Dad said quietly. 'We pass through the Lunar Curtain soon.'

We sat side by side as the ship zipped past the Seven Sisters, each planet suspended, one behind the other, and finally slipped satin-smooth through the Lunar Curtain. Five hours later, there was a fierce whoosh of energy and the star-ship locked on to the black hole known as Sagittarius, the central black hole of the Milky Way. Within minutes, we passed through the funnel that would lead us inexorably to the Shadow Planet's solar system. I looked at the Icarus Wall on my left. Through it, I could see the Shadow Planet, exactly as it had been downloaded to me: a spinning blue ball shining in the dark.

'It's beautiful, isn't it?' Dad said. 'So blue.'

I didn't say anything, though I had to admit that it looked pretty.

'It's the water,' Dad said. 'Seventy per cent of Earth is water. It's one of the reasons we chose it.'

'Earth? That's the only name they use, isn't it?'

Dad grinned across at me. 'Yes. They don't know that they are our shadow, our little laboratory, so they call the planet Earth. Only *we* call it the Shadow Planet.'

'Earth,' I said. 'I'd better remember not to call it anything else.'

'But, as I told you before, Aria, they are destroying their own environment,' Dad said. 'The atmosphere is heating up. Soon, they wouldn't be able to survive there – which is why we have to put a stop to them.'

'Why didn't we warn them, though, Dad? Seems a bit harsh to just wipe them out.'

'No point in warning them. They already know. They just aren't prepared to change their behaviour.'

I tried to imagine that. Were they crazy? Where did they plan to go when the Shadow Planet could no longer support them?

'Tell me what you know about them,' Dad said. 'I know you've been doing your research. I hear you're a bit of an expert.' He grinned at me then and I knew he was teasing.

'All right,' I said, putting my bad humour on hold. 'Ask me anything!'

'How long have they been there?'

'A thousand years approximately. They believe they've been there for hundreds of thousands of years, of course. That is what their history tells them, what the science tells them.'

'And in reality?'

'In reality, they only know what *we* tell them. We created them. We gave them their history, their archaeology, even their memories.'

'And they look like us?'

I knew that this was a trick question. I smiled. 'We created them in our own likeness. They are like we were a thousand years ago. They have the same DNA that we had a thousand years ago. Our DNA has changed, but they still look like us or like we did until we realised we prefer darker skin tones.'

'Go on – do they live in families?'

'They are social creatures. They live in families, but they don't have the same kinds of attachments that we have. They know from a very young age that they will die. Apparently, that doesn't encourage people to attach too deeply to one another or to the planet.'

Afterwards, I thought about humans again and the way they existed. How strange to live for such a short time and to know you would die. On my planet people didn't die of disease because years of research had given us immune systems that could fight off anything. When people reached their two hundredth year they usually left Terros and went to live in comfort on one of the Seven Sisters, so that Terros didn't get overrun. They could choose to continue working if they wanted to, but many people saw moving

31

to one of the Seven Sisters as a wonderful never-ending holiday, a reward for work well done during their lives on Terros.

We had also done work on our own genetic structure, eradicating the bad genes, fostering the good. Which is pretty smart when you think about it. Sure, we had to be careful about what we ate and how much exercise we got, but it was better than dying. And then my stomach twisted as a new thought struck me. Was my DNA a ticking clock that would stop after seventy, eighty, a hundred years, no matter what I did? I inhaled sharply.

'You OK?' Dad said, looking across at me.

I had to appear normal. Not let him see how I was feeling. I mustn't look in any way alien. Alien. An alien. That's what I was. I almost laughed.

'Aria?'

'Great,' I said. 'I'm fine. What time will we be there?'

'Soon,' Dad said. 'We are going to a city called Dublin. We chose it because it's one of the places where people speak Terrosian – though they call it English. Also, it's a small city, fairly easy to get around.'

'So that's where you will release the virus?'

'Yes. Dublin is near a country with a large population, so the virus will spread quickly. It's a mutated strain of the 787 flu. An interesting virus. It disguises itself in the body, presenting as an amino by-product. In that way it gets past the immune barrier and causes havoc. Seb has done a lot of work on it.'

'Will it kill?'

Will it kill me? That was what I wanted to say. *Will it kill my funny rope-ladder DNA?*

Dad shrugged.

'We don't really know what the first dose will do. It may kill some people. But it will prepare the ground for the next dose and that will purge the planet of all human life.'

I closed my eyes and thought about that. Terros would work at restoring the planet to full health once the humans were gone. Then, it could be repopulated and a new experiment set up, or maybe Terros would abandon it. It was so far away and it took a lot of resources to keep it going, resources that might be better used somewhere else.

But mostly I thought about what it meant for me. I wanted to see them for myself, the humans. Rio's words were still echoing in my head. She thought that they were filthy and stupid and I was sure she was right. But did they have any good qualities? I had good qualities. Didn't I?

My restrainer automatically tightened, squeezing my ribs and welding my body to the seat. And then we were falling, faster and faster, my breath being sucked from my lungs. Falling through the stars, headlong, with no safety net.

'Here we go!' Dad's voice was calm in my right ear. 'There's the beacon!'

I looked and saw a pulsating light filling Dad's screen. He'd told me about it before we left. Our people had left an electronic beacon that meant we could always find the Shadow Planet, even though it wasn't in our galaxy. And then we were falling. I felt my stomach lurch, my eyes bulged, and then my nose began to run. My ears were totally blocked and everything sounded as though I were under water. I gripped the arms of my seat so tightly I was afraid my fingers would break. And still we fell. Down, down, down. I closed my eyes and then, as though someone had yanked me by the back of the neck, the ship shuddered, tipped and stopped.

'We've landed.' Dad's voice, still calm and soft, whispered in my ear.

I knew then that the *Veres* had landed smoothly on the water, out in the cold sea, exactly as planned. I watched Dad, his hands moving from one screen to another while the feed from Terros poured out data. He made the adjustments, enabling the sleek star-ship to become a submarine, dive under the waves and power through the last part of our trip. After the teeth-rattling descent, I hardly noticed. We re-emerged in Rossport, a small fishing port over a hundred kilometres south of Dublin, according to my Icarus Wall.

'Why are we landing so far from Dublin?' I asked.

'It's a sleepy place. Less chance of anyone official noticing us.'

As soon as our star-ship came to rest, Dad pulled a suitcase on wheels from beneath a seat.

'Time to get dressed,' he said. 'Put your clothes on over your bodysuit.'

I did as I was told, my breath quickening with excitement. I pulled out the sweater and jeans I had been given. The sweater was heavy and warm at first, but my bodysuit quickly adjusted my temperature until I was comfortable again. The shoes were a different proposition. They were called trainers, Dad had said, and were tied on to my feet with laces. They felt heavy and clumsy and nothing like the slim boots I normally wore. I just hoped that I wouldn't fall flat on my face while wearing them.

Dad had put on his human clothes too, and now looked exactly like the images of humans that had been downloaded to my brain, in his dark suit and white shirt and tie. We alighted from the ship just as the sun peered over the horizon. The *Veres* submerged again, slipping silently into the water. I followed Dad up the rough stone steps that took us on to the quay, afraid to breathe even though I knew my body could cope with the strange atmosphere. I looked up but the sun blinded me with a harsh white light.

'Dad!' I gasped, my heart thudding.

'It's all right,' he said. 'The light is brighter, harsher, here. Close your eyes for a moment.'

I did as he said, and even with my eyes closed, the sharp light pressed on my eyeballs.

When I opened them again the light was still intense and the scene in front of me seemed to be swimming.

'All good?' Dad said. 'It's strange at first but your retinas will adjust.'

He was right. Already it was getting easier to keep my eyes open. Dad handed me a pair of dark glasses and I put them on. I was sure I looked ridiculous but there was nobody there to see us apart from a black and white cat who tilted her head to one side, observing us, then strode away.

I took a deep breath in, relieved that it didn't feel any different to breathing on Terros. I looked around. This was my first time on an alien planet. The scene before me was anything but alien. I took it all in. The grey rocks splashed with lichen, deep shadows at their base, the bone-white sand, ridged by the wind, speckled with wrack-weed, and beyond that, the intense blue-black of the sea. It was so like Terros. A mirror image almost. The light was strange here, though. Everything seemed hazy, less defined than at home. It was like a smudged watercolour, I thought, all molten sky and sea. And that wasn't the only thing that was different. The air was cold and damp. I felt the deep thrum of my bodysuit pulsing against my skin, regulating my temperature. There was no climate control on the Shadow Planet, I knew that. Air moved between bands of high and low atmospheric pressure; weather came and went as it pleased. The place was totally feral, just like Rio said.

As we walked along the quay, leaden clouds skulked across the sky and the wind was bitterly cold. But it wasn't just cold, it was strong, and you had to push against it as you moved. That was something I had never experienced before and I wasn't sure that I liked it.

'The train station is this way,' Dad said. 'Let's go.'

He took my arm. We hurried across the coastal path and through the deserted streets of a small village. I had no time to take in the details. It was just a blur of low houses with brightly painted doors, shops with cluttered windows, and parked cars encroaching on the footpaths, but it felt like we had just gone back in time. It looked like those grainy old pictures of Terros from a thousand years ago. Old-fashioned houses made from old-fashioned materials that weren't energy-efficient, cars that belonged in a museum, and uneven paths and roadways. Seagulls seemed to follow us, squawking and squabbling in the cold air. Wild seagulls. I'd read all about this, how birds were allowed to roam at will on the Shadow Planet. I had only ever seen seagulls on school trips to the nature reserves. My heart lurched as the big white birds ducked and dived over our heads, screeching like sirens. I threw my arm up to fend them off, making Dad laugh out loud. We turned a corner and I saw a sign for the railway station. A small group of people huddled near the door.

'Quickly!' Dad said, and we crossed the road, heading for the station. Inside, everything was quiet except for the tinny loud-speaker voice listing off stations in an endless monotone – and in two languages.

Dad saw my puzzlement. 'They speak mostly English, which is a form of Terrosian,' he said. 'But they have an ancient speech also that they use from time to time.'

I shrugged. Weird.

Dad headed on to the platform to wait for the train to pull in. I looked up and saw an old man approaching. I was shocked. I had never seen the effects of ageing up close and personal. The man's skin was like a map, cross-hatched with deep creases and fleshy puckers, and his eyes were wet. His mouth, which was missing some teeth, had fallen in. His long grey hair hung down almost to his shoulders. But it was the way he moved that most shocked me. His shrunken body constantly trembled as though the ground itself was quivering beneath him and his head nodded in time as though he were listening to some mad music. The train pulled up, but I didn't move. Eventually, Dad pulled my arm and we scrambled on, leaving the platform and the man behind us.

As soon as we boarded the train, I was hit by the foetid smell of sweat and damp wool, like the train had just woken up from a cold, deep sleep. Dad found us two seats together at the end of a carriage; he stood back and let me take the seat by the window. The throb of the engine rose and then the platform was falling away and the wheels of the train quickened.

I had downloaded information about trains, but that didn't give you the warm muggy smell or the wild rocking as the train moved along the metal rails. Dad had explained that people spent hours at a time getting from place to place. Strange behaviour for people who have such short lives.

I studied the dusty floor, the worn seat covering and the grime-streaked window. I was shocked at the turbulence of the train. No magnetism here, no metal floating above metal, with nothing but a positive/negative charge keeping them apart. The train was sitting on the tracks beneath, twisting and turning as it went, bucking, jostling, throwing the passengers about at will. No-one seemed to pay any attention.

Finally, out of boredom, I forced myself to look up. The first thing I noticed was the contamination problem. In the hour I had been on the train I had already seen five people coughing, two sneezing and one spitting something out of his mouth. Germs abounded and I could almost see the bacteria grow in front of my eyes. Rio was right. They were filthy. Were they not terrified,

I wondered, as the blonde woman opposite coughed again, sending a spray of spittle delicately through the air. Dad must have sensed my unease because he took my hand and squeezed it.

'They can't hurt you,' he said kindly. 'Your immune system is too strong.'

I wouldn't be too sure of that, I thought, but I said nothing. I glanced around the carriage again. There were lots of white people. I had never seen a white person in reality before. I had imagined that white people had white skin but they were more pink than white. Some people's skin was dotted with brown and others had red blemishes. I looked at my own brown skin.

'Why are so many of them white?' I said to Dad in a voice that only he could hear.

'In the beginning we had people of all colours on Terros too, but our forefathers soon realised that white skin has the poorest defences against radiation. That is why we are all dark-skinned now. But the white-skinned people here have been useful to us. We could continue to test the skin against sunlight and other dangerous substances.'

I eyed the woman sitting across the way from me. She was dark-haired with brown eyes and pale skin. I couldn't help thinking that she looked anaemic, less healthy somehow. The woman glanced at me and smiled. I looked away. It was hard not to feel sorry for her.

Outside the window, the fields and rivers of the Shadow Planet raced by. Houses dotted the landscape as though they had been thrown at random by a clueless giant. I couldn't stop a smile. Rio would say I was letting my imagination run away with me. When we were little, one of our first teachers used to read old fairy stories to us. Even then, Rio would attack them from a scientist's perspective, pointing out that there were no giants on Terros, no dragons and no witches. I, on the other hand, wanted to believe every word.

Through the window, I could see the cars and buses that clogged the motorways, belching their foul emissions into the atmosphere. I could almost see the temperature rising. What kind of place was this? How could I have come from here? At the railway station – Connolly Station it was called – I followed Dad through the throngs of people and into a taxi.

'Forty-five St Brigid's Road,' Dad said.

The driver was a white-skinned man wearing a peaked cap. 'Harold's Cross way?' he asked.

Dad nodded and we drove over a bridge and along beside the river.

'So, where are yous from?' the driver asked, as he pulled up at a traffic light.

There was a second of silence before Dad answered.

'India,' he said. 'But we have lived in London for years.'

I watched the man carefully. Did he believe us? Every atom in my body was poised to flee if he didn't.

'India!' the man said. 'Cricket, yous boys play, right? My brother-in-law – he's English – he plays cricket. I'm more of a soccer man myself. Liverpool. You folly the soccer at all?'

'As you say, we play cricket mostly in India.'

I clutched the silver memory disc hanging around my neck, reassured by the familiar sensation on my fingers.

The car went scooting through a slovenly world of garish bill-boards screaming their messages at me and empty spaces where tufts of wild flowers pushed up through blue-black tarmacadam. Tarmacadam was another human invention. I couldn't imagine wanting to pour thick sticky tar over the surface of your planet, smothering the grass and the plants. On Terros we walked over closely cropped herbs and scented flowers so that the scent wafted up as you walked. My favourite was the chamomile that was like a sponge beneath your feet, soft and bouncy, and when you stood on it its sweet smell filled your head. Everything here was so ugly. Scraps of paper, like injured birds, fluttered in the wind. I supposed people had just thrown them there, but why? I saw all the things I'd been told about flying by – shops, offices and schools. Finally the car pulled into a wide street, lined on one side with three-storey red-brick buildings, each with white windowsills. The windows on the upper floors had black-railed balconies. Trees, old and gnarled, flanked the footpath. On the opposite side was another line of houses with gaps between them like a bad smile. At the end of that row was a different type of building with a flat roof. It was five floors high, and Dad pointed it out to me as our new home.

The car stopped. Dad paid the driver. I climbed out of the car and looked around. Further on, to my right, down a winding hill, I could see a row of shops.

'This way. We'll take the lift,' Dad said, and we were moving again. Through the door, across a deserted tiled hall and into the lift. From what I could see, the lift was nothing more than a box worked by pulleys. Dad pressed the number three and the box lurched. Then, with a whine, it took us up three storeys. As the door of the lift opened we were almost run over by a young boy of about three.

'Upsadaisy! Upsadaisy!' he said, his face shining with excitement. 'Upsadaisy, Mama!'

He had soft brown eyes, I noticed. A blonde woman followed him.

'So sorry,' the woman said. 'He loves the lift. Megan!'

A young girl, about my age, came running down the corridor. She wore glasses and her blonde hair was scraped back from her face. She also wore an anxious frown. But it was the glasses that fascinated me. I could see that they were magnified to improve the girl's vision but the technology seemed ancient and the large-framed glasses made her look like an owl. On Terros we would have made sure that her vision was corrected while she was still an embryo, and if that hadn't worked, we would have fixed her eyes or grown new ones for her. All organs could be grown on Terros just by implanting DNA cells into a biodegradable plastic. It was elementary to my mind and I wasn't even good at science.

'Sorry, Mammy,' the girl said, stepping into the lift with her mother and the little boy, and then the door closed. I looked up at Dad.

'The girl has an eye malfunction of some kind,' he said. 'Probably a genetic abnormality.'

I nodded. 'Why didn't they fix it before she was born?'

'They don't have that technology,' Dad said.

I'd forgotten that. They had basic science and some technology, but not much. I waited while Dad chose a door, put a key in the lock and opened it. Inside was a brightly lit living room. Later, I discovered that the apartment also had a small kitchen, a bathroom and three bedrooms.

'It's very important that you stay inside,' Dad said. 'Until we leave, you only go out with me. You can't risk someone speaking to you. You don't know enough about the Shadow Planet to be believable. Do you understand?'

'Yes,' I said. 'Dad! Why didn't we give them the technology?'

'I'm sorry?' He was frowning.

'You said the girl was like that because of a genetic problem. Why didn't we give them the solution?'

Dad sighed. 'In time, we would have,' he said. 'But first we needed to see the effect of these problems to fully understand why things go wrong. That girl and others like her were observed, and data was fed back to Terros. In that way we were learning all the time.'

'But isn't that cruel?'

'It would be if they had feelings in the same way we do, Aria. But they don't. Their emotional system is totally compromised because of death. There's no point in worrying about them and they don't worry about themselves. They're born and they die. We use their lives, their data, to make our lives better.'

'You said earlier that the data is fed back to Terros. Who feeds it back?'

'Look out the window.'

I looked.

'See those birds? They are called pigeons. They are the receptors. Through them we have learnt all there is to know about the Shadow Planet. The people here ignore them. They are just part of the scenery.'

I stood at the window watching the birds, some on the ledge outside of the window, others on the street below.

Pigeons. I lodged the word in my short-term memory. Below me on the footpath, I saw the young boy from the lift walking with his mother and his sister. As I watched, the boy stamped his foot and a pigeon flew up, all wings and feathers, in a furious blur. The boy laughed. His mother took his hand and led him to the crossing. His sister glanced up at the window, and for a second I felt that she was watching me. The girl shrugged and followed her mother across the street.

5

I slept, eventually, in my strange bed surrounded by alien noises, the gentle thrum of the fridge, the ticking of the small clock on my wall and the occasional screech of brakes outside my window. In my dreams, I was back on Terros, swimming in the sea with my friends, hanging out with Mum and laughing at my own silly jokes. When I woke, my head felt heavy and my eyes were dry and uncomfortable. I sat up and looked around. I guessed it was late; I'd overslept. There was no Icarus Wall here, no comforting robotic voice telling me about the day ahead. Even the bathroom didn't work properly. I had used the toilet and turned to check for the analysis of my waste, but there was nothing there. No graph showing my sugar levels or whether I needed to hydrate. No faeces analysis reporting any unusual cell mutation. Nothing. The Shadow Planet, it seemed, was a high-wire with no safety net.

I stood at the kitchen door watching Dad. He didn't even notice me. He was pouring a clear liquid from a chrome flask into a plastic bag. His fingers were long and slim, his nostrils flared, his eyesight perfect. He sealed the bag with a metal twist and placed it on the table. I noticed how exact his actions were, his long fingers nipping and tucking. He was designed to be a scientist – anyone could see that. With a pang, I realised that I should have inherited some of that from him, and that I hadn't. I was awkward and clumsy by comparison. Was I even his child? He looked up.

'Is that the virus?' I asked.

Dad nodded.

'When do you release it?'

'This afternoon. On the DART.'

'The DART? A suburban train. Right?' I was remembering something from the Icarus Wall.

Dad nodded.

'Can I come?'

'Of course. You're my partner now, Ari.' He smiled. 'It's not as if the virus can hurt you. Your immune system is way too strong for that.'

We hope, I thought.

'But first, let's eat! I've had breakfast, but I'll have a snack with you.'

I watched as Dad put food on the table. It was all familiar to me. Water, apples and broccoli. I was just about to sit down at the table when I heard a knock at the door. Dad tensed. Another knock.

'Stay there!' he said, and strode across the floor. He opened the door and I saw the boy from the lift.

'Yes?' Dad said, his voice even, pleasant.

'Hello,' the boy answered.

Dad waited a beat but the boy didn't offer any more words.

'Can I help you?'

The boy didn't answer. He was looking at Dad intently.

'I'm sorry,' a girl's voice said. It was his sister. 'He didn't mean any harm. I was on the phone and I didn't hear him leave. He's absolutely impossible at the moment. Our mam's just gone to the pharmacy and …'

'It's perfectly all right,' Dad said. 'No harm done.'

'Come on, Ben,' the girl said, and then Dad closed the door.

I sat down.

'Let's eat,' Dad said again.

I wanted to talk about the boy and his sister but I knew that Dad was preoccupied. I decided to wait.

'When do we go?' I said when he had finished eating.

'Soon,' Dad said. He picked up a newspaper from the table. 'Help me with this,' he said now. 'It will take our minds off things.'

I leant over and saw a black and white box.

'It's a crossword,' Dad said.

I was vaguely familiar with the idea. Dad had explained it to me years ago. You got cryptic clues and tried to work out the answers.

'Try one on me,' I said.

Dad picked up the paper.

'Right. Five across. It's got seven letters. *A girl on each knee.* What do you think?'

Cryptic. I focused on the words. On each knee. What was the name of the bone in the knee? I scanned my anatomy download. Patella?

'Too easy,' I said. 'Patella – the kneebone, and the word is made up of two girls' names, Pat and Ella.'

Dad grinned. 'You are good at this,' he said.

We passed a pleasant hour finishing the crossword. Pleasant, because I was at least as good as he was at it, maybe better, once he'd explained some of the things to look out for in the clues, things like anagrams and hidden words. I really liked all the figuring out and had almost forgotten about our mission.

Then Dad stood up abruptly.

'Time to go,' he said. 'You need to get dressed. Take off your bodysuit – can't risk it being seen by a human – and put it in the bag. We'll leave it at a luggage storage place in the city centre. We'll get a locker there. It's all been arranged. That way, should anyone search the apartment, they won't find anything incriminating.'

It felt strange to be without my bodysuit, and the clothes were uncomfortable, scratching my skin, but I pulled them on and

45

took a quick look at myself in the mirror. I looked like a human, I thought, but nothing like myself. And I didn't feel like myself either. My suit had been a part of me from birth. Its sensors were connected to my neurological system and able to send signals to my brain. In that way my body was kept free from all bacteria and at a constant temperature. Now, without it for the first time, I felt out of control. My head felt warm but my hands and feet were cool at best. I brushed my fingers along my arm. My nerves tingled and a shiver rippled down my back. It felt strange to be in direct contact with skin. It looked so vulnerable. I tried not to think about what the sun would do to it, but the weather was very dull, I reminded myself.

'Aria!'

I hurried back to Dad. He looked at me carefully.

'You'll do,' he said with a grin. 'Follow me.'

Outside, we waited for the lift. It came trundling up to the second floor. Then it stopped. An older woman suddenly appeared beside me. She was small but hefty, with a doughy face. Her eyes seemed to bulge unnaturally and she had a thin pink mouth. She glowered at the lift.

'Stopped at the second floor as usual. That's those Reilly kids, always messing with the lift. I've told Mr Levi about it numerous times, but he doesn't do anything, does he? Visiting someone, are you?'

I looked at Dad with a raised eyebrow.

'No,' Dad said. 'We live here.'

'Oh?' the woman said. 'On this floor?'

'Yes. On this floor.'

'Oh, you must have moved into Fred's place. Number fifteen?'

Dad didn't answer her. The woman turned her gaze to me.

'You're in number fifteen, are you?'

I nodded.

'I'm across the corridor. Pender's the name. Missus.'

With that, the lift doors opened and we all stepped in. The woman didn't speak again, but I could see that she was scrutinising Dad under her eyelashes. I was relieved when the door opened and we parted company.

Twenty minutes later we were in the city centre, on what must have been the main street. Very wide with trees down the middle.

'The luggage storage place is just down this way,' Dad said.

We stopped at the entrance to some sort of shopping centre and went inside. I could see a glass-fronted unit with the words *Left Luggage* on a sign above the door. I waited as Dad spoke to the man behind the counter.

Minutes later we were standing at a bank of lockers. Dad chose one and put in the code he'd been given: 7964. I committed the number to my short-term memory in case I ever needed it. The locker opened with a click. Dad threw my suit and his own suit into the locker and closed the door, re-entering the code. With a final click, the metal box was locked.

I followed Dad then across a bridge over the river to the DART station. Tara Street the station was called. Or *Sráid Teamhrach* in the other language they used. I couldn't begin to pronounce it.

As Dad was getting our tickets, a tinny voice was reciting the rules of the place.

This is a safety announcement. It is not permitted to cycle, skateboard or rollerblade within the station building.

While Dad was busy, I examined a large poster on the wall, advertising a burger. It had a photograph of a round of meat between two pieces of bread. I knew about this. People on the Shadow Planet ate meat. Animals. It was an old experiment where scientists on Terros considered what would happen if food came from animals.

Rio did a project on it once. I remember her having a photograph of a rabbit on a plate surrounded by vegetables. Underneath it, Rio had scrawled: 'Hey, Mummy! I ate a bunny!' We were about ten years old at the time and thought it was really funny.

The scientists soon discovered that meat caused health problems, weakened the immune system and damaged the environment. Humans, however, still ate animals. What surprised me was that they knew all about the disadvantages, but continued to eat meat, because they wanted to, not because they had to. Weird. The voice spoke again.

Twenty-four-hour CCTV recording is in operation at this station for the purpose of security and safety management.

I looked around for Dad. He was coming towards me.

As we started up the stairs to the platform, I noticed a man playing a violin. I recognised the music at once. It was Mozart's Violin Sonata No. 27 in G, one of Mum's favourites.

'We gave them Mozart?' I whispered to Dad as we walked past the man.

Dad nodded.

'On loan. A few hundred years ago. They think he's from this planet.' Dad smiled. 'Best stay mum about that, I think.'

'Stay mum?'

'Stay quiet. It's a human expression.'

I shrugged. I couldn't imagine where that phrase had come from. I turned it over in my mind a few times and decided that I liked it. I glanced back at the musician. How little the humans seemed to like the music! They raced past the man, talking, laughing and ignoring the music altogether for the most part. I had to remind myself that humans didn't have the same emotional system, the same feelings. The music, though, was exactly the same, bold and brilliant.

The general behaviour of the people on the cold platform was more of a puzzle to me than anything the crossword had thrown up. The pushing, the shoving, the rudeness. Why did they treat one another so badly? Then the train came lumbering down the track, pulled to a stop and opened its doors. People piled out all hurrying away to somewhere else while we climbed aboard.

I watched Dad settle himself in his seat. He was carrying a briefcase and an umbrella. In his other hand was a folded newspaper. I had seen him place the plastic bag inside the newspaper before we left the apartment.

The carriage was full. I knew how Dad would release the virus but not when. Opposite me there was a woman with a black veil covering her face. I could only see her eyes. The veiled woman blinked and looked away. The train slowed. I looked at the display. It told me the next stop was Pearse. The train stopped then and the doors opened.

The veiled woman got out and a couple piled on with three young girls.

'Sit!' their mother said. The girls jostled one another for seats, then finally sat down. The train rolled on again. Their father took out a newspaper and began to read. I glanced at Dad. He was sitting quietly, looking straight ahead.

I couldn't help wondering about the girls. They seemed happy, I thought, watching them. Their three heads were close together, whispering. Every so often, a burst of laughter pulled them apart for a second and then they went back to their chat. Would they get sick from this dose? What would the virus do to them? My stomach tightened. I didn't want them to be hurt. They weren't like us, I reminded myself. Dad was a good man; he wouldn't hurt children.

Without my bodysuit, my skin popped out a cold sweat. They were just little girls. In my head, I could see the virus, disguised as

49

an amino by-product, slip past their puny defences, opening the door for the second dose. The thought unnerved me. *They don't feel emotions like we do,* I reminded myself again. *They know they are going to die even as young children. Think about something else. Think like a scientist.*

Across from me, a boy about my own age caught my eye. He had white skin and blond, almost white hair. He wore blue jeans and a T-shirt with *New York* written across it in red and blue letters. But it was his eyes that fascinated me – large blue eyes, blue like a summer sky, but flecked with grey. I'd never seen that before. Suddenly he smiled, and I realised that I had been staring at him. I looked away as the train stopped again and the doors opened. A few minutes later I glanced across at him again, and he was still smiling. I couldn't resist it. I smiled back.

Flustered, I looked up again at the display. Now it showed Lansdowne Road. I looked away and caught Dad's eye.

He looked at me and nodded. I stood up. As I did, I saw him leave the plastic bag on the floor and then kick it under his seat. He stood, and as the doors opened, he deftly punctured the plastic bag with a quick stab of his umbrella. I was already moving towards the door but I managed a quick glance back at the bag. I was just in time to see the clear liquid seep onto the floor. An innocent puddle under a flood of new feet.

6

Back in the apartment. I felt as though I had run a marathon. 'Adrenaline,' Dad said. 'It tires the body.'

I went back over all that had happened on the DART. There were many more sophisticated ways to release the virus, but Dad explained that all of our actions must look like they were human actions.

'That is how we have stayed undetected for so long. Everything we have done could have been done by a human. If the police find evidence, it will be evidence of human terrorism, not alien action.'

I wondered if people had already contracted the disease. We knew that the human immune system wasn't very strong.

'When they get the virus ... will they suffer? Before they die, I mean.'

I studied Dad's face to see how he would react to my question, but there was nothing, not a flicker. He was as calm as he always was.

'No. They don't experience things as we do, Aria. You know that.'

Did I know that? Did he even know that for sure?

'Will their immune system ever improve?' I asked.

'Of course,' Dad said. 'They are already living longer than they used to. They don't help themselves, mind you. They are being manipulated by nature, by the animals they rear. Humans like the taste of meat so they eat flesh. They need more and more meat so they keep more and more animals. That's good for cows or sheep,

51

as it ultimately guarantees the survival of their species, but not so good for humanity.'

'And we know that meat isn't good for us or them.'

'No, it isn't,' Dad said. 'It clogs the arteries, which causes heart disease, but it also causes big problems for the planet. Cattle emit methane. Methane contributes to the greenhouse effect, which is causing serious climate change and destruction of the environment.'

'And they *know* all of this?'

'Yes. You know how at home we have made a commitment to protecting our environment and ourselves? They haven't done that on Earth. Not yet. Or not properly anyway.'

Mention of the environment reminded me of Rio. I wondered how she was getting on. We had no way to communicate and I missed her. She was passionate about protecting not just Terros but all of the neighbouring planets too.

Dad stood up and turned on the television.

'I told you about this. It's a sort of entertainment system,' he said, as he flicked through the channels. He stopped at a national news report. 'This is a news programme. It tells you –'

Suddenly, he stopped talking. A young woman was standing outside Lansdowne Road station, a microphone in her hand. I stared at the screen. The voice was ordinary, colourless.

There was a major emergency this afternoon on a train at Lansdowne Road DART station, when a man was observed in an alleged chemical attack. A young man travelling on the train saw what appeared to be an Asian man in his thirties leave a plastic bag on the train, which later turned out to contain a toxic substance.

A photograph flashed up on the screen. It was the boy with the strange eyes, the boy who had sat opposite me, who had smiled at me. My heart skipped a beat. This was my fault. All my fault.

He was the one who had noticed what Dad did, because he had been looking at me, and I had smiled at him.

The woman on the screen was still talking.

The chemical is now being examined and a task force has been set up to interrogate witnesses and search for clues. The Taoiseach appealed to the public to co-operate with the investigation and help apprehend the culprit. The gardaí appear concerned that the assault may not be the last, and they have stepped up security at train stations and airports around the country and are inspecting all railway platforms for suspicious objects.

Some of the words I couldn't understand. 'What?' I said. 'Who?'

'Prime minister,' Dad said. 'Police.'

I didn't hear any more after that. Blood was pounding in my ears. Dad was standing immobile, watching the flickering box in the corner. The remote control fell from his hand.

'We have to get out of here,' he said, but I wasn't heeding him.

After the guards had finished searching for clues, troops trained in chemical-warfare procedures cleaned up the train and the DART station. They wore gas masks and full protective bodysuits and used special solutions to neutralise the chemicals.

'Aria! Now!'

He was in the bedroom but I couldn't move: I was glued to the television screen.

The newscaster continued.

Passengers travelling on the southbound DART this afternoon between twelve thirty and two o'clock are asked to contact their nearest garda station. A manhunt is now underway.

Dad was already moving, throwing things into his large bag.

'We have to get out of here,' he said. 'We'll make our way back to Rossport and be out of here within twenty-four hours.'

I nodded, but inside something felt all wrong. What would happen if the humans caught us? Would they know we weren't from this planet?

'Do they know … at home … about this?'

'Of course,' Dad said. 'The data will have been fed back.'

'Will they send help?'

Dad looked away. 'We won't need help,' he said.

The word *manhunt* had lodged in my brain, like food caught between the prongs of a fork. Were they already hunting?

'Start putting your things away,' Dad said, as he picked up random pieces of clothing from around the room. His movements were quick, deft, like a bird's. My own body felt leaden, as though there was a weight on top of my head. Nonetheless, I did as I was told, though my mind was racing.

What if we were captured? Earthlings didn't believe that there was any life in the universe apart from themselves. Why had I smiled at that boy, encouraged him to take an interest in me? He hadn't mentioned me to the police, I realised. He had only spoken about Dad. The guilt was like acid, and my stomach hurt.

A knock on the door startled us. The knock was followed by the sound of a girl screaming. Dad dropped his bag and went to the door. The voice was crystal-clear now.

'Help me! Please! Help me!'

It was the girl from the lift, tears streaming down her face.

'Please,' she said. 'It's Ben. There's something wrong.'

She caught Dad's hand and pulled him towards her. I followed them.

The girl lived in the apartment next door. As I went through into the living room I saw the boy. He was lying on the floor, his face white, the skin around his mouth tinged with blue, and he wasn't moving. Dad picked the boy up as though he weighed nothing and put him on the sofa. He opened the small mouth and peered down his throat.

'What happened?'

'He was eating an apple and –'

Before the girl could finish, Dad caught the boy, put him across his knees and turned him over. With the heel of his hand he hit him a hard blow between his shoulder blades. Instantly, a lump of apple flew from the boy's mouth and he started to cough. Dad stood him up. Tears streamed down the child's face as the coughing intensified, but colour was flooding his cheeks and he was swallowing large mouthfuls of air. The girl seemed paralysed at first, then she grabbed the child, hugging him and crying herself.

'He was choking,' Dad said. 'The apple was blocking his airway.'

The girl left the boy and looked up at Dad.

'Thank you,' she said. 'I didn't know what to do. He's never choked before and my mother is out and –'

Dad touched her arm gently.

'I have to go,' he said. 'I have a plane to catch.'

'I'm sorry. You're in a hurry. My name is Megan, by the way, and this is Ben.'

Dad shook her outstretched hand. 'Lucas, and this is my daughter, Aria.'

I took the girl's hand. It felt warm. Megan looked back at her brother.

'He'll be fine now,' Dad said. 'Nothing to worry about.'

The little boy had finally stopped coughing. He stood watching us for a moment, then turned and lay on the sofa, his back to the room.

'We must go,' Dad said, and took my hand. Megan was still thanking us as the door closed and we hurried back to our own apartment.

'As soon as you are ready, Ari, we'll leave,' Dad said.

'Are you sure?' I said. 'Maybe we should lie low until things die down. Are they still talking about it on that television thing?'

We both turned to the box. The woman was still there. She looked more anxious now. A frown creased her face.

We have unconfirmed reports of early casualties amongst the passengers who were on the DART stopping at Lansdowne Road this lunchtime. The affected people are reporting severe headaches, fever and in some cases a raised red rash.

Dad switched off the set.

'Hurry, Aria! We need to go. Get your things.'

I got as far as the bedroom door before I started to feel unwell. There was a strange ache in my chest and my skin felt too hot. I took a deep breath. My knees buckled. One minute I was standing, the next I was falling until my knees hit the floor, pain coursing through my body. From a long way off I heard my own voice.

'Dad!'

The word echoed and re-echoed, but I couldn't grasp it. Couldn't hold on to it. Then Dad was beside me, lifting me up before I sank into a pool of black.

7

Time seemed to stop then. I didn't know how many days I'd spent in the dark hole. I only remember Dad's voice coming from a long way off, the sharp prick of a needle in my arm and mad dreams like information surges with no words, only images.

In my dreams, pigeons as big as mountains flew about my head and planets reduced to the size of crumbs cavorted in a grey sky. I knew that I was creating the images, forming them from memory and imagination, but I had no control over them. They galloped away from me when I tried to grab them, leaving me feeling exhausted and powerless. I moaned. I could feel Dad holding my hand.

'Aria!' His voice came from a long way off.

I struggled to open my eyes but they were too heavy.

'Aria!'

This time I managed to push up my weighted eyelids. An image swam in front of me, zooming in, then zooming out again. A man with a beard. A stranger in our apartment.

'Dad!'

The word formed in my brain. I felt it in my mouth. I prised my parched lips apart, tried to speak, but no sound came out. Again I shaped the words in my brain, feeling the vowel on my lips. *Da...*

Summoning all my energy I tried again.

'Dad!'

This time I heard it. I didn't recognise my own voice. It was hoarse, raspy, but it got a response. The bearded man squeezed my hand, then stroked my head gently.

'Aria! You're awake. Don't try to talk. Just lie still. You are in the apartment. You have a drip in your right arm. You've been unconscious for a few days, but you are safe now. I'm going to prop you up.'

He had Dad's voice. Strong hands grasped my shoulders, pulling me forward. I could feel him packing pillows behind me, and then I could see the room.

'Do you think you could eat a little, sweetheart? Rachel next door made soup for you. Carrot and coriander. You like that? Just try some.'

He was gone and I could hear the clattering of pots and the hiss of gas. I licked my lips. They were dry and had tiny slits in them that hurt. I tried to imagine eating, but I didn't feel hungry. I rolled up one sleeve of the shirt I was wearing and looked at my arm and saw a tiny pinprick red rash. I stroked it. Tiny bumps. Alien bumps. Something had breached my defences. My mind imploded. *The virus.* My immune system had been bypassed. Would I die?

'Now, Aria,' the man with a beard said. It was Dad, but with a beard. 'Try this!'

He held out a spoon, putting it close to my mouth. I could smell the carrot. My stomach lurched.

'No!' I managed to get the word out.

He put down the bowl. 'It's all right, Ari,' he said. 'Give yourself time.'

I looked at my arm. Touched it.

'You've seen it,' Dad said, his voice even. 'It is a virus. *The* virus. It found a way past your defences. But don't worry. We can fix this. We just need an antidote. We need to find one, and then … and

58

then … we'll rebuild your immune system. You will be as strong as ever you were.'

'I … I won't … d-die?'

I heard the short, sharp intake of breath. 'My poor baby,' he said, and I could hear the emotion crackling in his voice. 'Of course you won't die. I would never let that happen. I don't understand why your immune system didn't recognise the virus.'

I could hear the guilt in his voice.

'It wasn't your fault,' I said.

My eyes closed and, despite my best efforts, I couldn't open them. I felt the pillows being taken away and I slipped into the black again.

The next time I woke, a girl was sitting in the chair beside my bed. A shaft of light from the window fell on her hair. It was Megan, the girl from next door. Where was Dad? Why was the girl here? I observed her for a few minutes. I had barely glanced at her the last two times we'd met and the first time all I saw were the glasses. She was reading a book. She was wearing jeans with a dark red T-shirt that matched her red-painted nails, and on her feet she had furry boots. She had three metal studs in her right ear and her skin was white – so white that it seemed to be translucent. As I watched, she looked up and I saw that she had wide-spaced grey eyes behind the glasses, soft eyes.

'You're awake, then? I'm Megan from next door. Your father had to step out. Shouldn't be long, I'd think. He doesn't like to leave you … Sorry! I'm rabbiting on. Like a drink?'

She lifted a glass from a table beside the bed. I scanned my body as I had been taught to do since I was a small child. Was I thirsty? Was it just a craving? I was thirsty.

'Please,' I said.

Megan helped me to sit up and held the cool glass to my lips. I swallowed the water thirstily.

'Do you remember what happened?' Megan said, replacing the glass.

'Not really,' I said. I had no idea what Megan knew or didn't know.

'Your father told us that you collapsed. It has to do with your blood condition. He thinks that you might have forgotten to take your medicine?'

Blood condition? My thoughts were racing. Dad must have invented some story about me having a 'condition'. I decided to say as little as possible. Megan didn't seem to need any answers. She was still talking.

'Could be worse. You could have got that virus the terrorists released on the DART. Did your dad tell you? It's some kind of flu. They keep saying they don't think it's that contagious because it hasn't spread much. Still, you get all the loonies who refuse to believe it. You should see Mrs Pender! Do you know her? Miserable bag. She lives across the way.'

'I met her at the lift once,' I said, remembering the woman with the small eyes looking Dad up and down.

'She's going round wearing a mask. Like a surgeon.' Megan laughed. 'No fear she'd get it. Not a bug alive would live on her, my mam says. My mam is Rachel. Have you met her?'

'No,' I said. 'I saw her once with your brother.'

'She's been helping your dad take care of you.'

'That is very kind of her,' I said, though I couldn't imagine this strange woman taking care of me.

'Well, she owes him. He saved Ben's life.'

The apple. I remembered that.

'You are lucky your dad's a doctor. At least he can take care of you.'

Dad must have said he was a doctor. What else had he said?

'Like to hear some music?' Megan said. 'Who do you like?'

My mind was blank. Who did I like? Rio and I listened to so much music.

'Mozart,' I said finally.

Megan grinned. 'Very funny! I'll play you some tomorrow, whatever you like. Here! I'll leave you my phone number. If you think of anything you want you can call me and I'll download it.'

She scribbled the number on a piece of paper and handed it to me.

'So who do you like, really?'

There was silence for a beat. I sensed that I was supposed to talk about music, so I changed the subject.

'More … water, please,' I said.

This time I didn't need to scan. I knew that I wasn't thirsty, but I needed to stop this conversation.

Somewhere, a door banged.

'Your dad's back,' Megan said, holding the glass for me again.

Dad came in, smelling of the outdoors, leaves and flowers and cold air.

'You're awake,' he said. 'Thank you, Megan. I'll take over now.'

Megan stood up. 'I'll bring music tomorrow.'

'Thank you,' I said, and then she was gone.

Dad waited until the door slammed behind Megan.

'We need to talk,' he said.

'Yes,' I said.

'But first, how do you feel?'

He sat on the chair beside my bed that Megan had just left.

'Tired,' I said. 'That's all. Just tired.'

'No pain? No nausea?'

I shook my head.

'I told Megan and her mother that you had a rare blood disease, to explain the drip.'

He pulled something from his bag and put it in my ear. It was a human device – a thermometer, I guessed. I wondered vaguely where he'd found it. It beeped and he removed it. I watched as he examined the reading.

'Still a bit warm but we are getting there.'

'When will I be better?'

The question had been bothering me for a while. I had never had my defences breached as badly as this before, and I had no idea what to expect.

'Not long. This stage won't last long.'

'This stage?'

'Yes. We designed this virus to work in two different phases. Remember? Stage one is a severe infection, reducing the body's defences. Not everyone who contracted the virus lost consciousness as you did, but some people did, and that was not expected. The people who were on the DART are shedding the virus all the time, so it is spreading through the community quickly. The government are telling people that it isn't particularly contagious because they can't see the symptoms. But even though most people don't show any symptoms, the virus has embedded. The body's natural defences should recover enough to deal with this first stage in twenty days, we reckon. People who have shown symptoms will start to feel better. Temperature will normalise. The rash, if present, will disappear, but the virus will continue to spread. The people who were not on the DART won't even know they are sick. Then we move to stage two. At that point, another team will come and release the second dose.'

A cold thrill of fear ran through me.

Dad stood up. 'You don't need to worry about that,' he said.

'You will be safe at home when that happens and we will have an antidote developed, ready to give you.'

'Will have? You mean you don't have one already?'

Dad shrugged. 'We never expected to need it, Aria. Of course we know exactly how to manufacture it. We just need the time to grow it.'

'Can we go home soon? I am strong enough, I'm sure. I could be if …'

Dad sat down again. He took my hand. 'I need to explain something to you, Aria,' he said. 'We can't go home as long as you have the virus. We have to kill it first.'

It took me a minute to absorb what he was saying. 'I can't go home?'

'Not until we kill this virus,' he said again, patiently, as though there was something wrong with my hearing.

'We can't bring an infected person back to Terros. You understand that, Aria. This thing breached your defences – who is to say it won't do the same to others on Terros? It would be a criminal act. You know how much time and sacrifice have gone into securing a powerful immune system for our people.'

I did. It hadn't worked for me, but then again I did have wonky DNA.

'I will go home,' Dad said. 'I'll grow the antidote. It should take no more than seven days. Hopefully, Seb has already begun the process. Then I'll come back for you. In the meantime, you stay here with Rachel and Megan. I'll tell them I have to go on a business trip. How does that sound?'

Unbearable, I thought, but I didn't say that.

'Seb? You told Seb Roy?'

'He's leading this mission, Aria. He was very understanding. He's known you all your life. He's going to help us.'

I tried to process that. I tried to believe that Seb Roy would help us, but my mind kept going back to the lab and his conversation with the other man about his campaign for leadership of Terros. I had never liked Seb Roy, and that night in the lab he'd seemed so strange, so driven. I wanted to tell Dad all about it, but something stopped me.

'It's going to be all right, Aria,' Dad said gently. 'Everything is going to be fine.'

'What will they think at home? Where will they think I am? Will you tell them I am … am … sick?'

He flinched, as though the word had hurt him.

'No,' he said. 'No-one must know that. I have told your mother, of course. No-one else will know.'

Apart from Seb, I thought. I caught my father's hand. 'When do you leave?'

I wanted him to go. He was a wanted terrorist. What if the police caught him?

'Soon,' Dad said. 'We need a cover story.'

Nothing about being an alien from another planet, I thought wryly.

'I need to know what music I am supposed to like,' I said, suddenly remembering my chat with Megan. 'Mozart doesn't appear to be what she was expecting.'

'Why don't you rest now?' Dad said, ignoring my question. 'Help your body heal. Do you need anything?'

I lay back down on the soft pillows.

'Can you put my disc in my ear for me?' I said. 'My shoulder hurts.'

'Of course,' Dad said, slipping the chain from around my neck. He removed the silver memory disc carefully and slipped it into my ear. I felt the familiar weight as it settled against my eardrum.

'Have a little trip down memory lane,' Dad said.

I closed my eyes. Our memory discs were one of Terros's greatest achievements. They were designed to de-clutter our brains: memories took up too much valuable brain space and so were stored outside the body. Tiny robots, nanobots, made from strands of DNA, swam around in the capillaries of our brains and created a storage facility. In the same way that using tools brought our ancestors to a new level, these nanobots bring us to another level.

As soon as Dad put the disc in my ear, I was back home, but not on Terros. On one of the Seven Sisters. Rion, the one furthest away. We were on holidays, me and Mum and Dad. I was about eight years old.

There was rarely time to enjoy such memories. It was something to do when there was nothing else to do, and there was always something else to do. Now, I let myself stay in the dream state, enjoying the moment. It was like watching a familiar, comforting film.

We were walking in a valley. Above us, purple mountains loomed and beside us a stream raced towards the sea. My eight-year-old self stopped to gather bluebells. Dad laid a rug on the ground and unpacked our picnic. I could feel our sun warm on my skin as I slipped into a deep sleep, my memories still playing softly in the background.

When I woke again the light had faded. Dad sat at the table, writing.

'Ah! You're awake!'

I slipped the disc from my ear and put it back on the chain. He hung the chain about my neck.

'I have been preparing a backstory for you. I think I've covered everything. You like Ed Sheeran by the way.'

'That's what? A band?'

'No,' he said. 'A singer.' He smiled. 'You don't need much. I'll be back in a week. I've kept it simple, much the same as it always was. You were born in northern India in a city called Jaipur. It's in the district known as Rajasthan. Your first language is Hindi but you have forgotten it because you only speak English at home. If you don't have a perfect English accent that is why, though honestly, your accent is neutral, so I don't think they'll notice. You have been living in London, since you were five. I am a doctor, here in Dublin for a conference. Your mother is dead. You are Hindu by religion.' All of this was what we had prepared. 'So here's what's new. You have a blood condition, a type of cancer. You were diagnosed last year and had chemotherapy. You made a good recovery but you have to take medicine every day and sometimes you forget.'

So far, so plausible. Mind you, I couldn't imagine someone forgetting to take medicine that was keeping them alive, but I let it go.

'I've made a list here of books you've read, music you like, et cetera.'

I glanced at the page and sighed. Downloading directly to the brain was so much more efficient and so much faster. I tried to think of anything else I would need to know.

Dad had turned on the television. I looked up at the box. The young woman was back, only now she was in a studio, looking straight at the camera.

The Minister for Health, Daniel Harrison, today told the Dáil that he now believes the chemical left on the DART was more than likely a flu virus. This strain of flu has never been seen before in this country, but is believed to be relatively benign. People who were affected initially are now making rapid recoveries with no obvious long-term consequences. He stressed, however, that there is no room for complacency. Flu is a serious and potentially life-threatening illness. The virus is also very transferable, with cases having been reported as far away as London in the last twenty-four hours.

And they know nothing about phase two, I thought.

'Anything else you think you might need to know?'

Everything. I needed to know everything but there was no time. A knock on the door stopped me mid-thought.

'Megan?' I said softly.

'Perhaps,' Dad said, but he frowned.

I heard him open the door and a male voice speaking.

'Good afternoon, sir. My name is Garda Joe Dowling and this is my colleague Garda Fiona Rowan from Pearse Street Garda Station. We're investigating the recent terrorist attack on the DART. Could we have a few moments of your time, please, sir?'

'Of course,' Dad said, though I could hear the underlying tension in his voice.

'You are Dr Rega. Is that right? We got a list of names from Mr Levi, the landlord.'

'Yes,' Dad said. 'That is correct.'

'And your home address?'

'I live in London.'

'Are you here alone, sir?' the officer asked.

If they came in, they would see me. They would know I had the virus. They would know we had been on the DART. Why had Dad set up my bed in the living space? I tried not to move, to quieten my breathing.

'My daughter is with me, but she's out shopping at the moment.'

'You didn't happen to be on the southbound DART last Thursday by any chance? The one that had to terminate at Lansdowne Road.'

'No,' Dad said. 'I was not. I don't like public transport. I prefer to walk when I can. I was shopping that day, as it happens. In Brown Thomas, on Grafton Street, looking for gifts for my family.'

'I see,' the policeman said. 'That's nowhere near Lansdowne Road, of course.'

'But as I said,' Dad interrupted, 'I didn't take the DART.'

The woman spoke. 'Can you remember what time you got back to your apartment?'

'About six, I think.'

'Well, thank you for your time, sir. Enjoy the rest of your trip.'

The door closed again. I released the breath I had been holding.

'Did they believe you?' I asked as soon as Dad reappeared.

'I don't know,' he said. 'They are suspicious because they are searching for someone Asian and they think I look Asian.'

'Because of the colour of your skin?'

'Yes, and some people with light skin are prejudiced against people with dark skin anyway.'

'Oh! Why?'

'It's hard to explain, but over hundreds of years, people on Earth came to be classified by skin colour. Of course, that classification system was decided on by ONE group ...'

'Well, that's not very fair!'

'Lots of things on Earth aren't fair, Aria.'

'Will the police come back?'

Dad shook his head.

'I don't think so. We can take down your drip today. The rash is already receding.'

I felt the small pinch of the needle being removed from my arm. I did an internal scan. No pain. No fever.

'What about the people next door? Won't they tell the police about me?'

'No,' Dad said. 'I asked Rachel not to say anything. I explained that the authorities would not like me taking care of you at home. They would want you in a hospital. I didn't want that. I explained that you were delicate. I was worried about cross-contamination.'

'And she agreed? Even though you look like an Asian man and that is who they are looking for?'

'I saved her child. She is grateful. That will sustain her for the moment. Later, she may have doubts, she might contact the police, but by then it will be too late.'

I could imagine that. The 'terrorists' from next door would just have vanished – and Megan, Rachel and Ben would be dead. The thought made me feel ill. I had to keep reminding myself of all I had been taught about them: they didn't form close relationships, they weren't emotional in the way we were, they didn't love like we did. It was confusing, because Megan looked and sounded just like me or any of my friends. I pushed the thought away.

'Can I get up today?'

'I don't see why not. I think I should leave tomorrow, Aria. How do you feel about that?'

I felt terrible. I wanted to get away from this place. For once, I gave in to it.

'Please,' I said, 'take me with you.'

Dad shook his head.

'You know I can't do that, Aria. If there were any other way …'

I could see the pain in his eyes.

'I'm good,' I said. 'You go tomorrow. I'll be fine.'

8

The morning came sooner than I wanted it to. Light crept in through the blinds, playing on my eyelids. Before I opened my eyes I checked my body. All quiet. No pain. No fever. I couldn't relax, though. There was always the second dose. Dad had said that the second dose would be released later – that had been the original plan. Would someone from Terros release it, even if I were still here on Earth? What if I was already dead by the time Dad got back? They were questions with no answers, so I left them. Besides, I had more immediate problems.

Dad was leaving today. I would be left here – far, far away from home, on a tiny planet in the Milky Way. I saw an image of myself as a shadow, thrown against the blue of the Earth.

'Awake?' said Dad.

'Yes,' I said, 'I am.'

'I'm nearly ready to leave, Aria.'

'Wait,' I said. 'I'll get up.'

I didn't want him to leave while I was still lying down. It would make me feel too vulnerable, too weak.

In the kitchen, he was drinking water. His bag was on the floor beside him.

'I will leave you this,' he said. 'It's a communicator, looks like the mobile phones they use here, but you will be able to send me messages on it and receive messages from me. It uses Earth's own satellites, but we have adapted their technology so that now we can send messages much farther. We won't be able to talk, but you can write to me. Look! I'll show you.'

For the next few minutes he explained the device to me – how to send and how to receive, how to power it up, how to fix it if it malfunctioned. I found it hard to concentrate. Hard to commit to memory. I wished it were a straightforward download, whereby I would find the information neatly filed in my brain whenever I needed to retrieve it. The virus had left me feeling woozy. My thoughts were like mice, scurrying about with nowhere to hide.

'Do you understand?' Dad's voice cut through my rambling thoughts.

'Yes,' I said. 'I think so.'

'Don't use it unless you really need to,' he said. 'This technology is not something we want to draw attention to. I will never use it unless it is an emergency.' He smiled. 'Now, money!' He pulled something from his pocket. 'It's a lot more than you will ever need but it's better that you have it. I've put it in this wallet. I'll leave it here. OK?'

He put the wallet into the cupboard with the cups and plates.

'OK,' I said.

'I'll be back in a week. Nothing for you to worry about.'

'Tell Mum that I miss her.'

Why had I said that? The words had just tumbled out, bypassing my filter altogether.

Dad smiled. 'Of course. See you in a week. Oh – one last thing.'

He thrust his hand into his coat pocket and pulled out a small black box. He handed it to me.

'What's this?' I said.

'Just a precaution,' he said, but I noticed that he couldn't meet my eyes. 'It's a tablet called diocysterin.'

Dio. The second-chance pill. I'd heard about it. It was for people injured in accidents, something like that. I concentrated on what Dad was saying.

'Only use it if your life is in danger.'

'What does it do exactly?' I said.

'It will reboot you. It will heal you, but you can only ever use it once.'

'In your whole life?'

I had never seen Dad look so serious. This time his eyes met mine.

'In your whole life,' he said.

Why had we never discussed the magic pill before? What else had they not told me? He squeezed my shoulder.

'You are going to be fine, Aria,' he said. 'Think of this as an adventure. Imagine the stories you'll have for Rio.'

His eyes were soft and I could hear the slight break in his voice. I knew that he was as worried as I was.

'Go!' I said. 'I need my beauty sleep!'

I made myself smile and he threw his arms around me and held me close. And then he was gone.

I looked at the box with the magic pill and picked it up again. I opened it. The lid gave a satisfying click as it sprang back. Sure enough, inside was a single purple pill. I took off the chain that hung around my neck and removed the memory disc. The disc was housed in a type of locket and I was able to open the back panel and put the pill in. It would be safe there. If I was still here when they released the second dose, I could take it. At least I wouldn't die – even if I was left on a planet full of dead bodies. An image flashed into my head of a trail of destruction with people dead on the streets, in their houses, in the parks. I pushed the image away.

I felt strange now that Dad had left, untethered, as though I could just float away and no-one would ever miss me. I wasn't from here. I couldn't get back there. For the first two days I didn't go out; instead I slept a lot. On the third day I woke early, consumed by loneliness. Dad would be home by now. The word *home* made my eyes fill with tears. Why had I let him go? What if he never made it back? I shook myself. I couldn't succumb to these dark thoughts. I would write. Mum always told me to write when I felt stressed.

'You are more relaxed when you're writing,' she'd said.

I took out my notebook. Dad had bought it for me here in Dublin. We had writing technology at home that didn't involve paper, but I preferred the oldest way of all. I liked to write the words with a pen directly into my notebook. I placed my pen on the white paper and focused. For some reason, the image of the Shadow Planet as I'd seen it from the *Veres* was what came to me.

I opened the book and began to work. I wrote about seeing the Shadow Planet for the first time, its curves, the cobalt blue of it and the white of the swirling clouds. Soon I was lost in churning tides and wild birds and before I knew it an hour had passed. My shoulders started to ache. This surprised me because my muscles were strong – they didn't normally ache. I assumed it had to do with the virus. I stopped for a minute, laying down the pen and stretching the muscles in my neck, and suddenly the room felt like it was closing in on me. I had to get air.

I went to the window and looked out. The day was grey. Across the road, a solitary flag blew in the wind. I pulled on my coat – soft blue, made of wool, with black shiny buttons. I would walk, breathe cold air and smell the outdoors. Guiltily, I remembered Dad's warning about staying inside. But it was too much to ask, to expect that I would stay cooped up in here. I had money and

I could buy fruit at the shop and come straight back. I waited at the lift. The doors opened and Mrs Pender stepped out. She was wearing a mask, just as Megan had said. I almost smiled.

'It's windy out there today,' Mrs Pender said.

Her voice sounded muffled inside the mask. I said nothing. She stepped into the box and pressed the button. The foyer was empty. I pushed the big glass door away from me and stepped on to the street. It was windy and cold. A pigeon stood on the path, pecking listlessly at a piece of bread. He looked up as I passed, head on one side. I wondered if he was recording me. The thought made me feel uncomfortable.

I pulled my coat closer to my body. The smells were overpowering: food, smoke and something else. I sniffed the air. Rain. The weather here fascinated me. On Terros all weather was planned and manipulated by meteorologists. If rain were needed, clouds were allowed to form, and if it were not needed, clouds were blown away. Wind was only ever a soft breeze. But here, weather was random. How did they cope with that? How did they ever make plans? As I walked, the wind seemed to blow harder and soon I felt cold drops of rain on my face. I hurried on.

I had no problem buying the fruit, if you call tired apples and a dehydrated-looking orange fruit. The man in the shop was brown-skinned like myself. He was friendly and smiled at me as he talked. The newspapers all had the same headline, something about a war in Ukraine. The scientists on Terros were enthralled by the way Earthlings still waged war. On Terros war was an almost prehistoric concept. It was hard to imagine that it would ever be a real option. But on the Shadow Planet, the humans continued to kill one another to solve problems. These were people that didn't live long and yet spent time and energy on waging wars.

Go figure! I decided to do some research, try to figure it out from a human point of view. I hated being here, but I could make good use of my time.

It was raining heavily by the time I got home. My hair was wet and clung to my skin, which had pushed up little bumps – goosebumps they were called. I had been briefed about this – but it was still amazing to see them. It was like my skin had suddenly developed a mind of its own. A shiver rippled through me. I still hadn't got used to that either. I knew it was a form of temperature adjustment where tiny sensors in your skin send messages to your brain, telling it to warm up, but every time it happened I smiled and wanted to share it with someone – Rio preferably. I knew she would love it, and that it would make her giggle, in that explosive, snorting way she had when something unexpected happened. I wondered where she was now and if she was thinking about me. She would be horrified to think that I was stuck on the Shadow. I shivered again. I needed to take better care. Those sudden adjustments would weaken my immune system. Even though I was no scientist, I understood that.

I was just drying my hair with a towel when I heard a tentative knock followed by a voice.

'Aria! It's me, Megan!'

I opened the door.

'I didn't know if you were up or not. Were you out? You're all wet!'

'Yes, I went to the shop.'

'I hope you don't mind me dropping in?'

'I'm happy you called.' I was surprised that it was the truth. I was happy to see Megan.

'I just needed a break. Ben is being difficult again.'

'Sorry?'

'They call it the terrible twos, even though he's three! Be grateful that you don't live with a toddler!'

I felt like I had missed some of the conversation. Ben? Her brother. I remembered that.

'I brought you some music. Your dad told me that you liked Ed Sheeran, so we could listen to some of that, if you'd like?'

Megan put a small speaker on the table and selected something on her phone. Instantly, the apartment was filled with sound. The singer had a really melodic voice and there was a driving guitar. I loved it. We listened to a couple of tracks and then Megan played me some of her favourite band. They were called Coldplay, and I liked them too. But it wasn't till she put on the last track that I was really transported. It was an artist called Bruce Springsteen, and his voice sounded like it was reaching into my heart. Megan played a piece called 'Dancing in the Dark', and we started to dance. Megan was a crazy dancer and just threw herself into the rhythm, arms flying, head bopping. I couldn't help laughing.

'What?' she said. 'Are you laughing at my dance moves?'

Before I could answer, she threw a cushion at my head. I picked it up and threw it straight back, and then we were both laughing and out of breath from the wild dancing. I don't know when I had so much fun. I didn't want it to end.

'That was the last thing my dad said to me before he died,' Megan said. '"Keep on dancing." It was the best advice I ever got.'

I could see the emotion in her eyes. I didn't know that her dad was dead. That was so sad. So unfair.

I was about to say something comforting when I heard a noise. *Ping!*

Megan looked at me. 'Is that your phone?'

She turned off the music. I was about to say that I didn't have a phone when I heard it again.

Ping!

The noise was coming from across the room. On the table was the communicator Dad had left me. The device we had agreed not to use unless absolutely necessary. I picked it up and hit the green button. I stared at the words on the screen.

'Is everything all right?' Megan said.

I looked at the words again.

1 down: The end result is what confuses the gander.

'No,' I said. 'I mean yes! It's fine. Just a note from my dad.'

Inside, my thoughts were colliding, scrambling, crawling around my head. Something was wrong. Something was very wrong.

9

As soon as Megan left, I set to work on the message Dad had sent me. At first I found it hard to focus. All I could think about was him saying that he would only contact me in an emergency. What had happened? Why had he changed his mind, and why was he sending me a coded message? I looked at it again, trying to steady myself.

1 down: The end result is what confuses the gander.

Well, '1 down' probably meant I was to read the message as if it was a crossword clue. And the word *confuses* was what Dad called an *indicator*, a signal often used in these puzzles. So I knew there was an anagram – a word whose letters could be rearranged to make another word. I examined the clue again. *The end result?* Maybe that meant the end of the phrase? So the last word was possibly the anagram. I wrote G A N D E R in my notebook and started to play with the letters.

Andger

Nerdag

Garden

No, I didn't think that was it.

Dan…

And then it struck me. Danger! *Gander* was an anagram of *danger*. Dad's message was simply *Danger*!

He was trying to warn me, but about what? Should I answer him? Maybe not, that was what he'd said. Better to wait. Maybe there would be more messages.

It was hard to stay still and do nothing with my foot twitching as though it wanted to get up and run, but I forced myself to do just that. The day dragged. I was brushing my hair when I heard the knock on the door. I opened it cautiously. Megan stood there with Ben by her side.

'Sorry to bother you, Aria. Would you mind if I left Ben with you while I go to the shop? Mum has been delayed and I need to get milk.'

I looked at Ben, who was playing with a button on his sweater.

'Of course,' I said. 'I'll watch him.'

I'd never looked after anyone in my life, but how hard could it be?

Megan's face lit up with a smile. 'Thanks, Aria.'

She dropped down in front of her brother. 'Ben! I want you to stay with Aria while I go and get milk. OK?'

Ben looked up at me and nodded. When Megan left I noticed that Ben had a book in his hand. He gave it to me.

'Read,' he said. 'Read story.'

I took the book and sat on the couch. He pushed his little frame right in beside me. Feeling him like that, the heat from his body against my side, was strange. But strange in a good way. I opened the book and began to read.

'Once upon a time –'

'No!' Ben's voice had a sharp edge to it. 'Read the witch!'

I looked at him blankly. I had no idea what he meant. Was this some kind of local slang? Was I supposed to know? I handed him the book.

'Show me,' I said. 'You show me.'

He grabbed the book and began to rummage through the pages, muttering under his breath.

'Here!' he said. 'Read the witch!'

I looked at the page he had chosen. There was an illustration of an old crone with grey hair and big gaps where her teeth should have been. I began to read:

The witch tutted and muttered and looked down the well.
Then she opened her mouth and laughed,
A laugh that frightened the birds,
Who rose in the air with a flap and a yell,
And the sky clouded over and the first raindrop fell.

'Again!' Ben said, rocking gently where he sat.

'Really?' I said. 'Wouldn't you like to hear the rest of the story?'

He looked up at me with big brown eyes. 'Read the witch. Again!'

He closed his eyes. OK, I thought, *whatever you want*. I picked up the book again and started to read. Gradually Ben relaxed. I felt the weight of his head on my shoulder. I looked down and he snuggled closer. I smiled at him and he smiled back, a slow, sleepy smile. I read the piece about the witch several more times before Megan returned until it became a kind of mantra. All the time Ben listened, sometimes saying the words along with me. Once, he stroked my cheek, rubbing his finger along my skin from behind my ear to the tip of my chin. I studied him, trying to figure out what was happening in his head.

'He had you reading the witch?' Megan said when she came to pick him up.

'Why does he like it? Why does he like to hear it repeated?'

Megan stroked the little boy's head.

'I have no idea,' she said. 'He's in his own world. Tomorrow it could be something else. That's what three-year-olds are like.'

I kept thinking about Ben long after he had left. He was such a beautiful little boy. And then I remembered the virus. Ben, along with Megan and all humans, would be wiped out. In my mind's eye, I could see Megan dancing, her face alight, and it made me feel strange, like I'd done something wrong.

And then another thought popped into my head. I might never see Dad again. Where was he now? What had happened? What did his message mean? It made no more sense than Ben's witch looking down the well.

It got dark early and I went and stood on the tiny balcony off my bedroom window. The sky was cloudless, lit by an enormous moon and a vast helter-skelter of stars. The Milky Way looked like a raggle-taggle explosion. It was nothing like the ordered arrangement of stars that trooped past Terros and the Seven Sisters.

I had fallen from a great height, and ended up here, in this alien place, with no way of getting back to where I'd come from. I was the girl who had fallen to Earth.

There it was again. That nip of loneliness that felt so weird. Reluctantly, I went back inside and closed the door, cutting off the noise of the traffic.

I was just about to fall asleep when I heard it again: *Ping!*

I almost fell out of the bed in my hurry to get to the device. I hit the button. The message flashed up.

5 across: Don't go inside claim umbrella now.

I grabbed my book and pencil.

Inside. That could mean that the solution to the clue was actually there, *inside* the clue. Usually it meant that the letters from the end of one word joined up with the letters from the following word to make a new word. I screwed up my eyes and examined the clue carefully. I couldn't find anything like that. Small bubbles of panic filled my stomach. *Stay calm*, I told myself. You can do this. I looked at the first words again:

Don't go

I wrote *stay* on the pad. Stay what? Stay there? No. I couldn't find *there* in that sentence. *Claim umbrella*. There it was! Mum! Last letter in *claim* meets first letters in *umbrella*! C*laim* **umb**rella. *Stay mum!*

Yes! My heart picked up tempo. I still wasn't used to that, my heart just doing things of its own accord with no bodysuit to regulate it. I turned my attention back to the clue. Dad wanted me to stay quiet. Not to contact him. Now the entire message read:

Danger! Stay mum!

What was going on? Dad obviously thought someone could overhear our messages. Someone on Terros? Probably. My head started to ache and I knew it was from tension. I needed to relax or the stress would damage my immune system. I knew exactly what to do, but I didn't want to leave the message from Dad. I wanted to keep thinking about it, checking that I had the right answer.

I sighed then and gave in. I had to take care of my body first. I sat cross-legged on the floor and tuned into my breath. Slowly I reined in my thoughts. A sense of peace descended and I stayed there for another hour, my mind blank, my body in a state of deep relaxation. I got up then, crept into bed and slept.

In the morning, I looked at the clues again, reassuring myself that I had got it right. I knew there was a problem, knew that I had to stay quiet, but it didn't explain anything. Finally, I couldn't bear it any longer. I decided to go outside and walk in the air.

I opened the bedroom window and stood on the tiny balcony. The morning was grey and moody, still sulking after the heavy rain that had fallen during the night. On the street below, I watched the cars swishing by, spraying the air with murky water, while the pedestrians on the footpaths dodged the puddles and stood in to let the cars pass. I thought it was funny, like they were doing a dance, trying to stay dry. Up over my head, there were patches of clear blue sky too, and even though my nose was filled with the biting smell of fumes, the wind was gentle and I liked the feel of it on my skin. Once I saw that the weather was in a peaceful mood and probably didn't plan to drown me, I got my coat and headed out. I was locking the door behind me when a voice stopped me.

'Hello!'

I turned to see Mrs Pender watching me.

'Yes?' I said.

The woman looked over her shoulder for a second, reminding me of a nervous lab rat.

'Is your father in? I was hoping he would join the residents' committee.'

Her watery eyes peered at me over a white surgical mask.

'No,' I said. 'I am living alone.'

The woman laughed, more of a cackle than a laugh, I thought.

'A bit young for that I would have thought!'

'I mean, my father is away on a business trip.'

I felt quite proud of myself. I'd remembered the cover story and delivered it so naturally.

The woman frowned. 'How long will your father be away?'

'I don't know. Maybe a week,' I said, wishing she would go away.

'What age are you?'

'Fourteen,' I said.

'Fourteen! And he's gone and left you here all alone. How will you eat? Do you cook?'

I shrugged. 'No,' I said. 'I eat fruit and vegetables. And seeds for protein.'

'Well, that's the best ever,' Mrs Pender said, but I thought she was possibly being sarcastic.

'If you will excuse me,' I said, 'I need to go out.'

The woman's eyes narrowed.

'Where are you off to?'

'Oh, just out for a walk,' I said, hoping that I sounded casual.

'I don't think that's a good idea,' Mrs Pender said. 'Not a good idea at all. Wandering around Dublin. A young girl like you? Better you stay indoors.'

I decided not to argue with her.

'What did you say your name was?' she said.

'I didn't say,' I replied. 'But it's Aria Rega.'

The woman looked me up and down slowly.

'Aria Rega.'

I waited.

'Best get indoors, then,' Mrs Pender said. 'Too dangerous to be out there roaming the streets.'

I opened the door and went back inside. I leant on the door and waited till the woman had left. Why did she care what I did?

10

An hour later I was ready to go out again, but this time I had a plan. I'd found a dusty tourist guide in the second bedroom and in it a map of Dublin and a transport guide. It was a really annoying way to get information, but I didn't have the kind of computer they used here to access the thing they called the Internet. I decided to go to a park and have a look around. There was a nice big one not too far away, though a bit far to walk, I thought. I took the money Dad had left for me and set off. It felt good to be independent again. I waited at the bus stop until the bus came. I sat at the front, behind the driver. The very idea of a driver made me smile, as all transport at home was run by artificial intelligence. Even my bike had a mind of its own. It seemed like a stressful job driving the bus, weaving in and out of heavy traffic, but the driver was relaxed, singing away to himself as he drove. Fifteen minutes later, I saw the gate to the park.

I strolled across a green lawn and sat beside the lake. I looked up at the sky and followed the journey of the clouds above my head. These were standard old cirrocumulus, wispy like tufts of hair, racing across a vivid blue background. The air was cold and crisp and the wind ruffled the fallen leaves every so often, sending them whirling along the paths.

If I listened hard, I could hear bird song, song that was familiar from the nature reserves at home, but different too. I could definitely hear the robin and another bird that I didn't recognise, but above all else, I could hear the pigeons. I'd almost forgotten about them. The perfect spies – there all the time, almost invisible, and all the time collecting and reporting. I shivered.

The lake opposite was mesmerising; the colour of the water was in a constant state of flux, probably because of the Shadow Planet's changing weather patterns. Edging the lake was a sparse line of trees and shrubs; some tall, some short and squat, reminding me of a line of people waiting for a bus. The tall trees were bare, their brown branches held out like they were begging us for something, while the short ones were evergreen, rounded and flouncy in their emerald outfits. On my own side of the lake, weeping willows bowed down to the wind.

I felt my body relax. My mind was totally focused, my heart-beat slow. I let my memories have free rein – the ones from earlier childhood that were still held in my brain. Walking in a field of bluebells at home, my mother singing in the background. The smell of wild honeysuckle and cherry blossom in the little wood we liked. On a day like today, we would let the pod ramble where it would. Our house would bounce gently along, suspended above the ground, heated by our sun. I sighed.

'Aria!'

The voice startled me. I looked up to see Megan smiling at me.

'What are you doing here?'

There was a smile on her lips but I felt that it was forced.

'I've been buying plasters,' Megan said. 'Ben fell in the play-ground this morning when I was supposed to be minding him. The local pharmacy was closed, so I thought I'd come into town for a change and take a shortcut through the Green to the bus. I love it here.'

She held up a box of plasters as evidence.

'I feel so guilty,' she said. 'I should have kept a closer eye, but he loves to climb at the moment.'

She glanced across at me and smiled again.

'I'm sorry,' she said. 'I am going on. It's just that he drives me crazy. But he's also adorable; I hate to see him hurt.'

'I'll go home with you,' I said, and started to gather up my things.

We walked together across the park and made our way to the bus stop. After a few minutes, the bus pulled in and we got on.

I knew humans didn't form attachments like the people on Terros, but it struck me that Megan *had* formed an attachment with Ben. Ben had formed some kind of bond with me even, when we were reading the story together. And then a darker thought struck me. What would my new friend think if she learnt the truth? My people were planning to annihilate all of them. I tried to listen to what Megan was saying.

'I don't have school this week. It's the October break. And we're getting an extra week this year because part of the school roof fell in. Are the schools in London closed as well?'

'Yes,' I said, hoping she wouldn't ask me any more questions. I wasn't that used to lying and didn't think I could keep it going for long.

'I might come over and paint your nails, if you'd like? I got a present of a manicure set for my birthday. It's really cool and has loads of different shades. There's sure to be something to suit you.'

I looked at my nails. They'd never been painted. It might be fun. Something else to tell Rio about.

Before I could reply, Megan's phone rang. I watched her take the call. Her long blonde hair fell across her shoulder and her skin looked whiter than ever against the black phone.

'I'll call you back,' I heard her say. 'We'll sort this out. Don't worry.'

'Everything OK?'

'It's a friend from school. He's in a bit of bother. I'll help him sort it out.'

I looked out on the street. People were walking along the path talking and laughing. They were so innocent. And then, out of the corner of my eye, I saw him. I jumped in my seat.

'You OK?' Megan asked, but I ignored her.

There! I could see him clearly, a tall man in a grey overcoat. I recognised the shape of his head, the way he walked with a slight bounce, the floppy hair. Seb Roy! It was Seb. My heart soared. Seb had come to get me. I had to get off the bus. I jumped up, almost falling over Megan.

'Aria! What is it? You look like you've seen a ghost.'

'No,' I said. 'Nothing like that. I don't even believe in the supernatural. It's just someone from home. I want to try to catch him. I'll see you later.'

And then I was running down the stairs of the bus, on to the path. Once there, I stopped and looked around. Where was he? How could I have lost him? And then I saw him again. At a junction, a couple of hundred metres from me, turning left. I started to run, scuttling between the people who littered the path, looking for open spaces. I dodged women with buggies, I skirted huddles of men standing around and smoking and I kept running. All the time, my eyes scanned the road ahead. I saw the lights change at the intersection and saw Seb cross the street. I picked up the pace. I never saw the beggar sitting on the path, his legs stretched out in front of him. My foot caught his ankle and I flew through the air, landing hard on my knees. Pain shot through me. The beggar stood up.

'You all right, love?'

I didn't wait to answer him. Seb! Where was he?

This couldn't be happening. He was gone, and meanwhile blood was pouring down my leg: bright blue alien blood dripping onto the grey pavement.

11

Back in the apartment, I bathed my cut knee. It hadn't been easy getting home without drawing attention to the fact that I had the wrong colour blood, but everyone seemed to be in their own world that day, and no-one noticed. The skin had a ragged tear and my blood, now blue-black, oozed from the cut. If I was human, I wondered, why didn't I have the same colour blood as humans? Yet another question that I couldn't answer.

I tried to be logical. Something was terribly wrong – Dad's cryptic message had made that clear. He must have sent Seb to help me, and he would have told him where I was living. But what if Dad hadn't managed to get that information to him, and Seb was in Dublin with no idea how to track me down? I couldn't risk him heading home without me.

I took out the guide to Dublin. On the little foldout map I located the street where I had seen him. Camden Street. It was mostly shops and restaurants on that street, but there were hotels around there too; I could see some of them marked on the map. I was pretty sure he had turned left just beyond the bus stop where I got off. He was probably on his way back to his hotel.

I took out my notebook and made a note of the hotels. He could be staying in any one of them. My brain told me that I was searching for a needle in a haystack, but my heart was optimistic. I would call to each hotel and ask for him. A sketch! I could draw a likeness of him to show people. I was good at drawing and I was fairly sure I could do an all-right sketch. Someone would recognise him and then I could leave a message for him.

I congratulated myself on being inventive. I couldn't help wondering what Rio would have thought of me. Thinking of Rio made me feel incredibly sad. I had to see her again. I couldn't believe that we might have said goodbye for ever. I had to find Seb and get home.

I wanted to go straight away, but it was already dark, and I didn't want to be found outside at this hour. From what Megan said, the adults here would notice someone of my age out alone. I would sleep and start fresh in the morning.

I woke as early morning light flooded the room. I ate a bowl of fruit and drank some water. I was about to leave for Camden Street when I heard a knock on the door. I hesitated. It could be the police again – or it could be Seb! I had to go for it.

Megan launched herself at me as soon as the door opened. A tall boy stood beside her, looking slightly embarrassed.

'I'm so sorry, Aria, but I need … we need … your help,' Megan said and walked in past me, followed closely by her companion.

The boy was white-skinned with brown hair. He stared at a spot beside his feet.

'Just hear me out,' Megan said. 'This is my friend Duke. Remember I mentioned him on the bus yesterday? He's in a bit of trouble and needs somewhere to stay. Just for a few days. Three max. Would you mind, Aria? I couldn't think of anywhere else.'

Did I mind? Wasn't my life complicated enough?

'Of course,' I heard myself say. 'He can have the back bedroom.'

Megan threw her arms around me. 'You're the best. Thanks, Aria.'

The boy looked up and I saw that he had vivid blue eyes.

'Thank you,' he said.

He turned and went down to the bedroom and I heard him close the door.

'I'm so sorry, Aria,' Megan said. 'I really am. I just couldn't think what else to do. He was determined to run away. His mother passed away three months ago and he doesn't have a father or brothers and sisters. He's been staying with his grandmother, but now his mother's sister wants to take him with her to Australia. He doesn't want to go, doesn't want to leave his granny. But of course he doesn't get to decide ...'

'That's terrible,' I said, and I meant it. Human life was so messy – there didn't seem to be any order.

'Did you catch your friend yesterday?' Megan said.

'Sorry?'

'The man you were chasing when you left the bus?'

'Oh, Seb? No, I didn't. I'm going to try to meet him later. In fact, I should go now, but you can stay as long as you like.'

Megan caught my arm. 'You are sure you don't mind about Duke?'

'Course not. He might as well use the place until Dad gets back.'

'He's really well behaved,' she said. 'He won't be any trouble. And I'll have to do your nails every day after this just to pay you back!'

Waiting for the bus, I played that scene over in my head. I knew that it had been a bit reckless to let the boy stay, but I didn't want to offend Megan. What harm could it do?

I got off at the junction where I'd seen Seb and turned in to the street where I thought he'd gone. The first hotel I came to had a large black door and a man in uniform standing guard. Was he some sort of soldier? Who knew! I climbed the three steps to the door, expecting the man to stop me, but he remained totally expressionless. My feet sank into the deep pile of the crimson carpet.

It made me feel as if I was sinking into the ground itself. Across from me was a long desk made of shining dark wood, with three young women standing behind it, all in navy and cream uniforms. One was dealing with a customer, one was on the phone, but the third one looked at me expectantly. She had thin eyebrows that looked like she'd drawn them on with a pencil.

'I'm looking for someone,' I said, pulling the portrait from my bag. 'His name is Seb Roy. He might be sleeping here temporarily?'

'I'm sorry,' the woman said. 'We can't give out information about guests.'

'Oh, please,' I said. 'It's very important. He's my uncle, you see, and I have to meet him today and I've forgotten the name of his hotel.'

The woman hesitated. She looked over her shoulder and then turned to her computer.

'Give me a minute,' she said.

I waited while the woman clicked and tapped on the ancient-looking computer in front of her.

'No, I'm sorry,' she said. 'We don't have anyone of that name.'

'Thank you,' I said.

I took the portrait and left. I repeated that performance in a few more hotels, all with the same result. Most wouldn't give me any information and those that felt sorry enough for me to look it up told me that he wasn't staying there. I was about to give up but I thought I'd try one more. The Beaumont. There was a tall thin man with a beaked nose at reception and I showed him the portrait.

'I'm sorry,' he said. 'I can't give out information about the guests.'

He must have seen my disappointment because he glanced into the foyer and turned back to me.

'See that elderly gent in there?' he said.

I followed his gaze and saw a grey-haired man with a walking stick sitting in an armchair reading his newspaper.

'He's here most days. He doesn't work here but he spends half the day there reading his paper. You could ask him.'

I thanked him and hurried inside.

He turned to the door behind him. I went straight over to the man.

'I'm sorry to bother you,' I said. 'But might you have seen this man? He's my uncle and I'm supposed to meet him.'

He took the drawing in his hands and held it close to his face.

'Let me see,' he said.

He took a few seconds to examine it and I held my breath.

'Yes!" he said. 'He comes in for coffee, like myself. They have excellent coffee here. He's been in every day for the last few days. Different times, mind you, not a creature of habit.'

I felt a strange fluttering sensation. I couldn't believe that I was excited at the prospect of seeing Seb Roy, but I was.

'Would you like to leave a message for him?' the man said with a smile. 'I can't promise anything but …'

'Yes,' I said, trying to keep my voice calm. 'I'll leave a message.'

The man rummaged in his pockets and produced a pen and a tiny notebook. He pushed the pen and paper towards me and I wrote:

Seb!

Please come and meet me. I am staying at 45 St Brigid's Road, near Harold's Cross. I need to talk to you.
Aria Evangular

Walking down the street after leaving the note, I felt as though a great cloud had been lifted from me. Seb would sort things out, and I'd be able to go home with him. I couldn't imagine what my parents must be going through.

I had forgotten all about Duke. When I opened the door he was standing in the kitchen and startled me.

'Sorry!' he said, when he saw my expression.

'I forgot you were here,' I said.

I regretted having let him stay in the apartment. I was certain that Seb wouldn't approve.

'Would you like a cup of tea?' the boy asked.

I shook my head.

'I'd rather water,' I said, taking off my coat. I was about to put down my bag when I heard it.

Ping!

Dad! I rummaged in my bag and pulled out the device. Duke was still talking, but I ignored him. I had to focus on the communicator. My hand shook as I opened it and saw that it was another clue:

Ye men are confused! Name hides in tree's ebony.

'Is everything all right?'

Duke was looking at me and frowning.

'Yes. I'm tired. I'm going to lie down,' I said.

He looked hurt but I didn't care. This message was all that mattered.

In the bedroom, I took out my notebook and pencil. I had to approach this logically, I told myself. I had worked out the others. I would work this out too.

Ye men are confused! Name hides in tree's ebony.

I could do this. I concentrated on my breathing. It took exactly two minutes and I had it. *Ye men*, I could see immediately, was an anagram for *enemy*. I moved on. *Hides* was an indicator. It meant that the answer was there in the words that I had, but hidden.

I concentrated on *tree's ebony.*

My heart raced. It was the *B* that gave it away. That, and the fact that I had been looking for him all day. I felt the blood drain from my face as I finally saw what my father had written:

Enemy Seb

12

Seb was the enemy – and I had given him my address. He would be here in minutes. But how could Seb be the enemy? Why?

The scene in the laboratory flashed before me. What had he been up to that night? He and the other man. The reality came in tiny bites, but it all amounted to the same thing. I had to get out of the apartment. I processed this information as I threw my belongings into my bag. My body meanwhile was going berserk. My pulse was racing and sweat tickled my skin. My head felt light. I had to get out of there. Get out before he came. But where could I go? Panic bubbled up inside me. There was nowhere to run.

I heard a voice in the living area. Megan. I had no time to talk to her. No time. But she came into my room.

'Aria?' Megan was frowning. 'What's the matter?'

'I have to get out of here.'

'You heard?'

'Heard what?'

'About the social worker? That's why I called. Mrs Pender told her daughter Evelyn all about you. Evelyn is a social worker and a busybody just like her mother. She's sending someone round to take you into protective custody till your dad gets back. I came to warn you.'

'Protective custody?' I had no idea what she was talking about.

'I don't know what the system is in Britain,' Megan said. 'But here, they don't like minors living alone. Once Mrs Pender told Evelyn that your Dad was gone, and that you aren't from here, Evelyn filed a report. They'll probably put you with a foster family and –'

'They can't,' I said. 'I won't go.'

'They won't give you a choice.' Megan's voice was calm but firm.

'I have to get out of here.' I tried to think. Where could I go?

Megan seemed to read my thoughts. 'But where will you go?' she said. 'You can't just wander around Dublin.'

'I don't know. Anywhere. I'll find something.'

I didn't know Duke had come into the room till he spoke.

'I know a place,' he said.

We both looked at him.

'You do?' Megan said. 'Where?'

'Oh, it's a few miles out of town. Abandoned.'

'You've been there before?' Megan asked.

'Once.'

'They wouldn't find me?' I heard the question come out more urgently than I had intended. In my mind, I was already there.

'They wouldn't,' Duke said.

'Slow down, guys,' Megan said. 'We have to think this through.'

'There is nothing to think about,' I said. 'Unless you know somewhere else we could go?'

I turned to Duke. 'Why didn't you go there when you needed somewhere to stay? Instead of coming here, I mean?'

He hesitated. 'It's boarded up. Falling down. I didn't fancy going back there.'

He looked at the floor.

'If it's all boarded up –' Megan began.

'There's a door at the side that opens if you kick it.'

I was already moving towards my own door.

'We need to leave now,' I said.

'I'll come,' Duke said. 'Let me get my bag.'

'You don't need to stay with me,' I said.

'It's not a nice place to be on your own,' he said. 'I don't mind staying with you, and anyway I'd like to avoid the social worker as well.'

'I'll go with you too,' Megan said. 'I won't stay but at least I'll know where you are.'

I put my own rucksack on my back. In it, I had put my few belongings and the money Dad had left for me. Duke got his rucksack, and the three of us headed out.

But as Megan turned the handle, someone pushed against the door. A woman stood there, wide shoulders, black hair. In her hand she held a briefcase.

'Ah!' she said. 'Are you Aria?'

'Run!' Duke said, and suddenly I was running, legs flying, arms swinging. We pushed past the woman and just kept going. Down the corridor. Forget the lift. Take the stairs. In the background, the woman was shouting my name. Beside me, Megan was panting, out of breath already. Down the stairs. Across the hall. Out the door. Across the street.

Minutes later we were sitting on a bus, Megan and I shoulder to shoulder and Duke sitting in the seat in front of us.

'Are you OK?' Megan looked at me.

I checked. My heart was slowing down and the knot in my stomach had loosened.

'I think so,' I said.

'Where are we going again?' Megan asked Duke as the bus moved away.

'It's west of here,' Duke said calmly. 'Can't remember the address, but I know how to get there. First we go into town, then we get another bus.'

'Are you going to call your father and tell him, Aria?'

I shook my head. 'I can't. There's something wrong with his phone.'

'Well someone else, then?' Megan persisted. 'An aunt? A friend?'

'There is no-one,' I said. 'Only me and Dad.'

Megan stopped then, but I sensed that she wasn't happy with my answer. I couldn't deal with that now. The important thing was to put distance between me and the social worker, and to leave Seb no clue as to where I had gone. Dad would be back any day, if things had gone to plan. In my gut, I knew that wasn't going to happen. Something terrible must have happened to him. Seb was here and he was the enemy. If only I knew why! He was going to be the next leader of Terros! How could he be the enemy? I would have to contact Dad, regardless of what he had said.

'Is it far?' I asked Duke when we'd been on the second bus for what seemed like hours.

'Three more stops,' he said.

Three stops later, we exited the bus and stood side by side on the footpath. Looking around, I could see that this was a quieter part of the city and more run-down. Without a word, Duke crossed the road and headed off, with Megan and me hurrying to keep pace with him. He stopped at the top of a long narrow street.

'Down here,' he said, and took off again. Minutes later, he pulled up outside the building he had been looking for.

It was the most curious building I'd ever seen. The facade had once fronted four shops, their boarded-up windows and doors still there, and above them, two more storeys criss-crossed with stout lengths of black timber. The crooked walls and dipping roof reminded me of the witch's house in Ben's fairy-tale book.

Megan looked up at the building. 'What a wreck!' she said.

'It's to be demolished to make way for a new road,' Duke said.

It started to rain. On the front door of one of the shops I saw a bright yellow poster. I went closer and read what it said.

DANGER

This structure is declared unsafe for human occupancy or use. It is unlawful for any person to enter or occupy this building. Trespassers will be prosecuted.

'Come round to the side,' Duke said.

The side of the strange building hunkered unsteadily over a narrow cobbled laneway. The cobbles were grouted with moss and weeds, and slippery from rain. Duke pointed to a small door in the stone wall.

'Stand back,' he said.

He gave a short, sharp kick and the door flew inwards.

'Come on,' Duke said.

The air inside smelt damp and mouldy. I held my breath at first, terrified of inhaling whatever it was that made the air smell so bad. Then I realised that I had no option and took a large gulp of air. I followed Duke across the dark hall and up a rickety staircase. At the top of the stairs, Duke turned right, down a long narrow corridor lined with doors. At the second door on the right he stopped.

'What is it?' I asked.

'We're going to the attic. It's where I went last time I was here. It's safer.'

We followed him through the door. At the far corner of the room was a set of steps leading to a trapdoor in the ceiling. Duke climbed the steps and I heard a sigh as the trapdoor was pushed up and a blast of cold wind assailed us. Megan followed him through the trapdoor.

When it was my turn, I carefully navigated the steps. Duke reached out his hand to pull me into the attic room. Then he closed the trapdoor. A sleeping bag was thrown on the floor amidst a pile of burnt-down candles. There was a grimy attic window that looked out on roofs and on the pavement far below. Then I saw that there was an almost invisible door, presumably to an inner room. It had no handle; just an outline showed that it was there. I pushed against it and it opened to reveal a second space. I was sure I could smell mould spores in the air.

'Home sweet home,' Megan said.

I shivered.

13

uke and I were alone. Megan had gone home with promises to be back in the morning with food. Before she left, I'd given her twenty euro for supplies. For now we had candles and matches as well as water and a bag of fruit. Duke had chocolate.

'Why do you eat that?' I asked him. 'You know there's sugar in it?'

'Of course,' Duke said. 'I like sugar.'

'But it's poisonous and highly addictive. We don't eat it where I come from.'

'Where's that?'

Damn! I'd been thinking about Terros.

'London,' I said, remembering the cover story.

Duke looked puzzled.

'They don't eat chocolate in London?'

'Yes,' I said. 'I mean … of course they do … but we don't.' What was I saying? He'd think I was mad. 'My family doesn't. My family doesn't eat chocolate.' The words were tumbling out of my mouth now and I could only hope that I was actually making sense.

'Is it a religious thing?' Duke said.

'Religious?'

What was he talking about?

'What religion are you?'

'Hindu,' I said. 'It is the oldest religion on the planet.'

He smiled. 'If you say so.'

'I do,' I said. 'Because it's true.'

'And Hindus don't eat chocolate?'

I gave up. 'It destroys your immune system,' I said, retreating to safer ground.

'Really? See that on the Internet, did you?'

Was he mocking me?

'No,' I said. 'My father is a doctor. Sugar is a poison.'

'If it were a poison, I don't think they'd let us walk into the corner shop and buy it. Do you?'

'It shouldn't be on sale,' I said. 'It should be banned.'

He put a square of chocolate into his mouth and grinned. 'But it isn't.'

'Don't you care that it is damaging your body?' I was genuinely curious now.

'No!' he said. 'I don't. I like it. Anyway, science is always getting things wrong. They used to say that meat was bad – now they say we need it for iron and things.'

'You don't. You don't need it at all.'

He sighed. 'Can we change the subject?'

'Of course,' I said. 'Why are you here?' As soon as I asked, I knew I'd said it too bluntly.

He looked upset. After a beat, he shrugged. 'My father died when I was a baby,' he said. 'My mother was all I had, apart from my granny. Mum died two months ago and I went to live with my granny. We were in a bad place, but we had one another. And then my aunt arrived. Carol. She lives in Australia, and she wants me to go and live with her there.'

'And your grandmother?'

'Carol wants her to come too, but that will never happen, which would mean that Granny would be left here all alone if I went. I can't do that to her.'

'So you ran away?'

'Yep. I figure Carol will get tired waiting and go home without me.'

'Why do you care so much about your granny?'

He looked at me strangely. 'That's an odd question. She's my grandmother! Why wouldn't I care?'

'Is she old?'

'Eighty next year.'

'People live less than that on average, don't they?'

'I don't know. I suppose.'

'So she will die soon,' I said.

'Don't pull your punches there, Aria. Give it to me straight.'

I didn't know what to say then. He hadn't given me any explanation, not really, but he was obviously attached to this old woman. And he had been attached to his mother, from what he said. I felt as if I had offended him. I watched him get up and walk across the floor. He took up the candles and matches.

'We should light these, maybe?' he said.

I nodded. He struck a match and held it to the wick. Even that small light banished some of the gloom. Within seconds, he had lit a circle of candles. Shadows sprang up on the walls and I found myself smiling. It felt cosy, somehow. I sat cross-legged and closed my eyes.

'What are you doing?'

'Meditating,' I said. 'I want to clear my mind.'

'Oh,' he said. 'Carry on, then.'

I closed my eyes again and concentrated on my breath, but images of Dad kept butting in. Where was he? Would he come back for me? If he did, how would he find me? I couldn't go back to the apartment. Seb would be watching. What did he want? I had messaged my father on the device, but it told me that my signal was blocked. Blocked! By whom? Why? It was no good. I couldn't relax. I opened my eyes. Duke was looking at me.

'My granny says the best cure for stress is a nice cuppa tea,' he said.

'Really?' I said. 'I'm afraid that's not true. Tea is a stimulant. It doesn't ease stress. You have to defuse it yourself.'

'Through meditation?'

'Yes.'

'And that obviously worked – so maybe we could try tea?'

He was so annoying. He didn't know anything, but he was so sure of himself. He stood up. 'Come on,' he said. 'There's a place down the street. It's nearly six. We'll get a hot drink and use the bathroom there. Bring a toothbrush.'

'You've done this before?'

He shrugged. 'I came here after my mother … after she … passed. I wanted to be alone.'

'But you went back?'

'I didn't want to leave my granny alone. It's hard for her.'

I couldn't imagine losing my parents. Mind you, until now, it wasn't something I ever had to worry much about.

'Come on,' I said. 'Let's have tea.'

Ten minutes later, we were ensconced in a small coffee shop. Our seat was an upholstered bench fitted into a bay window. There was a plastic cloth on the table. The woman serving brought us a metal teapot and two mugs. She was middle-aged, with greasy grey hair tied up in a pony tail. Her face was like a war zone, with deep lines around her mouth and eyes and brown teeth inside thin, pinched lips. She placed the teapot and the mugs in front of us. I noticed that one of the mugs was chipped. Duke took it. I couldn't help feeling relieved.

I knew that the piece of the mug that wasn't glazed would be swimming with bacteria.

'Anything to eat?' the woman said.

'No, thank you,' Duke said.

'Wait!' I said, as the woman turned to leave. 'Could we have fruit and vegetables, please?'

'Are you joking?' the woman said and her mouth twisted into an ugly sneer.

'No,' I said. 'I don't eat meat.'

'Good for you,' the woman said and turned to leave.

'Hold on!' Duke said. 'Could you make a banana sandwich?'

'I could,' the woman said. 'If I had a banana. We don't do fruit. This is a coffee shop not a green grocer.'

This is ridiculous, I thought, hunger gnawing at the pit of my stomach. 'You provide food for people and you have no fruit. How can that be?'

The woman turned on her heel and headed back to the counter. As she walked across the floor, I heard her mutter to herself: 'Foreign scum.'

Duke squeezed my hand. 'Take no notice,' he said. 'Finish your tea and we'll go.'

But I couldn't drink it. A lump had formed in my throat like a fist blocking my airway.

Duke paid for the tea. A man with a weather-beaten face took the money. The woman was nowhere to be seen.

We didn't talk much on our way back to the house. I was lost in my thoughts. I had felt real hatred from that woman in the café. I couldn't understand it. We were strangers to her. Why had she felt threatened by us? I didn't want to live with these people. I needed to get home. In my heart, I knew that Dad wasn't coming. I couldn't imagine what might have happened, but I knew I would have to get out of this place on my own.

'If you aren't white, some people here want to make you feel like you don't belong,' Duke said. 'Not just Dublin, actually – everywhere. Even if you are white, they can make you feel like that. I often feel like I don't fit in here either.'

Duke's voice pulled me out of my reverie. 'Why? Why do you feel you don't fit?'

You are human, I thought.

'After Dad died, we never seemed to have any money, even though Mum worked two jobs. You don't get rich working as a cleaner. Sometimes at school … I don't know … I just wished I was like the others. Our school was very traditional, middle-class. People had money. I got in there because Granny knew the principal, but I never belonged, not really.'

I thought about that. Something fluttered in my stomach, a feeling I had been trying to push away all my life. It had to do with Seb. He always made me feel like an outsider. He talked about 'we', but it didn't include me. I had tried to tell my mother once, but she said that it was a hormonal imbalance, that feeling of insecurity. It wasn't real. And maybe she had been right, but the feeling didn't go away. I didn't fit. The glitches. The breaches of my immune system. The time I got a common cold. The time I became allergic to dust. Nothing serious, but these things didn't happen to anyone else. I was human. I'd always been human. The Evaluator wasn't wrong.

'What's going on there?' Duke's voice startled me. A crowd of people were standing around a stand of free newspapers. A black board propped against it screamed the news.

First death from the DART virus! DART virus claims its first victim.

I felt the ground shift beneath me. I stopped walking.

'You OK?' Duke said, his hand on my arm.

'I need to get … get a copy.'

'Stay here,' he said.

I saw him approach the man and take the paper.

'Come on,' he said. 'It's cold here. You can read it at the house.'

I followed him. The rain had dribbled to a stop but the clouds overhead were dark and ominous. Dad and I had *killed* someone. Some people could die from this flu, Dad had said. The second dose would annihilate all of them. My mind busily processed the information, though my heart resisted it fiercely. *I* was going to die. I was going to die here, on a planet far from home. Even my heart knew there was no escaping that logic.

14

I slept fitfully. Duke had insisted I take the sleeping bag. He had bedded down on our coats in the inner room. Despite the sleeping bag, I had been cold all night and was glad when the dawn finally broke and a stream of weak sunlight came through the window.

I got up. I took my hairbrush from my bag and brushed out my hair. Later, I could go to a coffee shop and brush my teeth. The newspaper lay on the floor where I had thrown it the previous night. I picked it up and read it again.

A man has died following the DART virus, as it has become known. Many people developed mild to severe symptoms after the attack, but all of them seemed to recover within a few days. John Griffiths, a Welsh native, was admitted to the Mater Hospital. Dr Aoife Collins gave this statement late last night:

'It is with great regret that I must confirm that my patient John Griffiths has passed away. He was admitted earlier today with kidney failure. This is, it would seem, a further effect of the virus he contracted last week. Our sympathies go to his family at this difficult time.'

A man was dead. Dad had said he didn't think they would die after the first dose, but it was possible.

I was about to call Duke when I heard a noise downstairs. I listened hard, concentrating all my energy on that one task. There it was again. A footstep? Maybe Megan had come back. I decided to go downstairs. If someone had broken in, I didn't want to be trapped in the attic till they left. I opened the trapdoor and went quietly down the wooden steps. I crossed the floor. This was a bigger room with two windows onto the street. I waited. Footsteps coming along the corridor. Whoever it was, I had to confront them. I couldn't just stand here and wait for them to find me. I put my hand on the doorknob but at that moment someone pushed it from the far side. I stumbled backwards. The door opened and Seb Roy stood there, tall and thin as a twig, with the eyes that everyone noticed. Today they were sloe-black and looking into them was like looking down a dark well, so deep that you could never see the bottom. He smiled when he saw me, his thin lips wet, as though he had just licked them.

Enemy Seb.

How had he found me? He must have had access to all kinds of information I knew nothing about.

I took a step backwards. He closed the door.

'Well, Aria! Here you are!'

The same smooth voice. Nothing strange. Nothing to get excited about.

'What do you want?'

'I want you,' he said simply. 'I have business that needs completing, and you are crucial to its completion.'

I hated the way he talked.

'Where is my father? Where is Dad? Why hasn't he come back?'

'Ah!' he said. 'Your father is unable to travel at the moment. Parliament wasn't too happy with his mission.'

'What do you want?' I repeated. He ignored me. 'I know about my DNA,' I said.

He sighed. 'I was afraid you might. I suppose it was only a matter of time before you found out. It's natural for teenagers to be curious. But now that you know what you are … it's better for you … better for everyone …'

Now that you know what you are …

'What's better for everyone? Better if I'm dead?'

'There are worse things than dying. Trust me.'

'Why are you saying this?'

Seb sighed, then looked at me with his black eyes.

'You, Aria, are a mistake. You are, unfortunately, my mistake. An experiment I conducted fifteen years ago went wrong. I let sentiment cloud my judgement, which isn't something we scientists do very often.'

I was watching him carefully. If he once moved from the door I could make a run for it.

'Mistakes have to be fixed, Aria. You have to take responsibility for them and put things right. Lucas told me that you had contracted the virus. He was worried and confided in me. I thought it through and saw that this was the ideal opportunity to fix what I had done. But I can't be sure that the virus will kill you. So I thought it better to take direct action. It's all the same to you – your immune system has been seriously compromised, so you would never be allowed back on Terros.'

I forced myself to listen to Seb, though I wanted to spit in his face or kick him hard in the shins.

'I knew that questions would be asked. Up until now I have been the only scientist observing you. That would all change if you came back. And there are things about you, about what I did, that are best left unknown. Things that would endanger me, let's say, especially now. I intend to be leader of Terros and that means no loose ends. Nothing can stand in my way – no skeletons in the closet. Cleaner than clean – that is what Terros requires of its leaders.'

'Nothing like you then.' I spat the words at him but he didn't react at all.

'Where is Dad?' I said then.

'On Terros,' he said. 'Under house arrest and under twenty-four-hour watch, as is your mother. It seems that this mission of your father's had no sanction from parliament.'

'What do you mean? *You* sent him on this mission.'

Seb shrugged. 'Can you prove that? No. I didn't think so. This was something our government should have done long ago, but they hadn't the courage to carry it out. My friends and I decided to take direct action, and it would have worked too, if you hadn't messed things up.'

It was all making sense now.

'You tricked my father into doing your dirty work?'

'That's one interpretation,' Seb said, without a trace of remorse. 'The elders don't see it like that. They think your father acted alone and only admitted his crime because you fell ill.'

'All lies,' I said softly.

I wanted to hit him, to hurt him, to make him pay for what he did, but I forced myself to listen to him.

'It worked out very well for me. No-one wants you back, Aria. Not even your parents if they were honest.'

He moved from the door. I took one step towards it. When I looked up he was holding a revolver.

'I wouldn't do that,' he said.

From his pocket he took a metal bolt and slipped it on to the gun.

'A silencer,' he explained. 'Antiquated weaponry, but effective. Stand by the door.'

He moved to the bottom of the steps leading up to the attic.

'This way it will look like a human murdered you as you tried to leave. I'll call the police myself and report the crime. I have one of their little mobile phones. Now move!'

His last word galvanised me. I did as I was told. I watched his face as I shuffled to the door, my legs shaking, heart pounding. My parents would never know what happened to me. Rio would never know.

He raised the gun.

I barely saw the trapdoor open. Duke came from nowhere and, with a crash, flung himself on Seb's body. I heard the gun go off, saw a flash of light. The gun skidded across the floor.

While Duke grappled with Seb, I managed to pick up the gun. I saw Seb's fist slam into Duke's jaw. Seb raised his arm and hit him again. I heard a bone break. Heard Duke groan. Then I had the gun to Seb's head. I don't remember doing it. It just happened.

'Get up!' I said, rage coursing through my body like molten lava. 'Get up or I will kill you.'

Seb put his hand on Duke's chest; then he pushed himself up, putting all his weight on the boy. Duke groaned again.

'Get up!' I roared, jabbing Seb's skull with the gun.

Slowly Seb rose. I could feel my hand shaking.

'What are you going to do?' he said. 'Kill me? I don't think so.'

He took a step in my direction.

'Get back!' I said.

The words were barely out of my mouth when I heard the door downstairs open. Seb had heard it too.

'Aria! Duke!'

It was Megan.

Even as my brain registered that Seb was moving, he crashed into me with all his force, sending me sprawling across the floor. I managed to struggle to my feet and grabbed the gun again. Seb had disappeared. In the distance, I heard Megan scream. I raced for the door. Down the stairs, feet flying. Megan was standing in the hall. The front door flapped in the breeze.

'Is he gone?'

Megan didn't answer.

'Megan!'

'That's a gun in your hand.'

I was pointing the gun right at her. I lowered my arm. The weight of the gun seemed to drag me down.

'It's his,' I managed to say, as Megan pushed the door closed with her free hand.

'Who was that?' Megan said.

I tried to think quickly. 'I don't know. A thief maybe? He broke in and held me prisoner with the gun. Then Duke …'

Duke! I had forgotten about him. I turned and ran up the stairs, adrenaline rushing through me, blood pounding in my ears.

Behind me I could hear Megan. 'What's happened to him? Is he hurt?'

He was still lying there. He wasn't moving. I knelt beside him. Up close I could see the damaged tissue in his jaw already turning blue and swollen. I put my ear to his mouth. He was breathing. I suspected that his ribs were broken from the jagged sound of his breath. Was his lung punctured?

'Oh, my God!' Megan was beside me. 'What did he do to him?' She didn't wait for an answer. 'I'll call an ambulance. You stay with him.'

115

And then she was gone.

I stared down at Duke. Was he going to die? I already had the blood of one human on my hands. I felt his pulse, counted the beats and waited.

Finally, Megan came back. 'They're on their way,' she said. 'You'd better not be here when they arrive, Aria. The guards will be with them. I told them he was attacked.'

'But Duke didn't want to be found. His aunt will –'

'He has no choice,' Megan said. '*We* have no choice. We can't leave him like this, and we sure as hell can't fix him.'

I felt all the fight leave my body.

'What do I do with this?' I held up the gun.

Megan shook her head. 'I don't know. We should give it to the guards, I suppose.'

'Who?'

'The police. We call them guards or gardaí.'

I nodded. I'd heard that word before.

'Of course, your fingerprints are on it … unless we wipe them off?'

'It doesn't matter,' I said. 'They don't have a record of my fingerprints.'

'You're sure?' Megan looked at me strangely.

'Of course,' I said. 'What do you mean?'

With that, the ambulance siren screamed from the street, the blue light flashing through the window.

'Nothing,' Megan said. 'You'd better go.'

I turned and made my way up the wooden steps to the attic.

For the next while, I sat above the trapdoor and listened as Megan explained about the man, the attack and the gun. It all felt unreal. The ambulance men took Duke. I heard him moan as they lifted him.

'Duke!' A man's voice. 'Can you hear me?'

A beat. Then Duke's voice, weak and laboured but audible. 'Where's Aria?'

The door closed and they were gone. I climbed back down and stood in the empty room. A shaft of sunlight fell on something on the floor, something silver, shiny. I bent and picked it up. It was a memory disc. In panic, I reached my hand to my neck, but mine was there against my skin. This was somebody else's.

Seb! I was holding Seb Roy's long-term memories in my hand. I wanted to drop it, to put as much distance as possible between me and Seb Roy, but something made me hesitate. I shoved the disc into my pocket. I would think about it later.

Outside the window, a pigeon cooed. I looked up just in time to see a blur of grey feathers as it took off from the windowsill.

15

Seb would be back. He knew where I was. I knew that I had to get out of there. But where could I go? I paced the floor. *I have to wait for Megan*, I told myself. In the meantime, I could barricade the front door. There was a plank of wood in the attic. I could use that.

Minutes later, I had wedged the front door closed. It wouldn't hold for long but it would do for now. I sat in the hall waiting for Megan. The scene with Seb played on a loop in my head. I was human. My parents were under house arrest. Seb had conducted a mysterious experiment that had something to do with me. Bits of information, but no real story, nothing that tied it together. And then there was the virus. A man had died. Was I next? Without the antidote …

Ping!

For a second I didn't know what the noise was. Then it all came rushing back. The communicator was in my bag. I pulled it out.

Primarily rivers under Nantes.

This one was easy. *Primarily* meant I should take the first letters of the following words.

RUN.

Too late, Dad, I thought. *Where do I run to?*

I tried again to message him.

Signal blocked!

No way now of contacting him.

Megan's voice interrupted my thoughts. 'Aria! It's me. Open the door.'

I flung the piece of wood aside, the door opened and Megan came in.

'Come on,' she said. 'We'll get a cup of tea somewhere.'

What was it with these people and tea?

I nodded. 'How's Duke?'

'He's comfortable,' Megan said. 'His jaw is broken and a couple of ribs and of course there is the bullet wound, but he'll live.'

Relief flooded through me.

'Come on,' Megan said. 'I don't have long.'

I followed her. The coffee shop was called The Olive Tree. Two pigeons pecked at a piece of bread on the path outside the front door. Inside, Megan chose a seat near the window. It was cleaner and brighter than the coffee shop I had visited with Duke.

I shook my head. 'Not here.'

I chose a seat in a far corner, away from prying eyes. We couldn't be too careful now. I ordered tea.

'Where's your dad?' Megan said. 'Shouldn't he be back?'

'I don't know,' I said. 'I don't know when he will come. I haven't been able to contact him.'

'He's not coming back at all, is he?'

There was something hard in Megan's voice. Like metal filings.

'I … I really don't know.' What was I to say?

The waitress left the tea on the table. Neither one of us moved.

Megan leaned in closer. 'Stop lying. I know what you are.'

What you are. Not *who* you are. Time slowed. I saw the frown deepen on Megan's face and something develop in her eyes. Hatred? Anger?

'I don't understand …'

'I think you do. You're not who you say you are, are you? Your whole story is a lie.'

How did she know? How had she found out?

'No!' I said. 'That's not true. Why are you saying that?'

Had Seb told her?

I tried again. 'I don't know what you've heard, Megan, but it's not true.'

'Let's have a little quiz, then, shall we?'

'A quiz?' Was she losing her reason? *A quiz?*

'Question number one: where would you find Nelson's Column?'

I had no idea what she was talking about. Megan raised an eyebrow.

'No? Can't answer that?' she said. 'Let's move on. What about St James's Park? What city is that in?'

'I ... I don't know.'

'Funny that. Nelson's Column is in Trafalgar Square in London. Everyone knows that, actually.' She gave me a puzzled look. 'The park is in London too. I know. We went on holiday there last year. You don't know, though, do you? And you've lived there all your life.'

There was no way back from this. I looked away. I couldn't meet her eye.

'You've never been there, have you?'

I shook my head. No point in lying now.

'You're a terrorist. You and your dad are behind the attack on the DART. I'm right, aren't I?'

No mention of being an alien. Be grateful for small mercies, I told myself. But I had to convince her that I was innocent.

'Not me,' I said. 'I had nothing to do with it. Only my father.' I saw the sharp accusatory light in Megan's eyes dim a little. 'Really?'

'Yes. Really. I had no idea what he planned to do.'

'And he's dumped you now? Left you here to face the music?'

Something in Megan's words stung me. Maybe it was true. Maybe he had dumped me. Tears filled my eyes. I looked away.

A few seconds later, I felt Megan's hand on mine.

'I'm sorry,' she said. 'It's not your fault. I'm just angry.'

'I understand,' I said. And I did.

'It's just … he seemed like such a nice man. How could he have done this? How could he have hurt people like that?'

I shrugged. Megan was getting upset.

'And look how he's treated you. What will you do?'

'I don't know,' I said, glad to be able to tell the truth.

'Will you go back home? Wherever that is.'

I shook my head. 'I need somewhere to stay until I decide.'

'Half of Dublin is looking for you. Social Services came to the flat and found you'd gone. They talked to the guards. Then they did a background check on your dad and they couldn't find any trace of him. Do you know where he is?'

I hesitated. I had to tell her something. 'He's … he's gone home,' I said finally. 'I was too sick to travel. He said he'd be back in a week.'

'But he hasn't come?'

I shook my head. I didn't have to feign distress now. My heart was breaking.

'I will help you, Aria, but you have to tell me the truth. OK?'

I nodded. If only I *could* tell her the truth. People always asked for the truth, but sometimes they didn't know what they were asking for.

'The man who broke in and hurt Duke? He's a terrorist too?'

I nodded. 'He tried to kill me.'

'I know. Duke told the guards.'

121

'I don't know what to do, Megan. I can't stay at that house now.'

'No. You can't. Duke has had an idea.'

'Yes?'

'I don't know how smart it is, but he was insistent. You can stay at his grandmother's, just for a few days.'

My heart swelled. Why would Duke do this for me?

As if she had read my mind, Megan went on: 'You helped him when he needed it. That's what he said. He comes home from hospital tomorrow, but you can stay there tonight.'

'Thank you,' I said. 'I'll never forget his kindness.'

Megan frowned. 'It's just for a few days, Aria. We can't go on like this. You're going to have to turn yourself in.'

'I know. Just not yet. OK? I need time to think.'

'And what if that man comes after you again?'

'He won't find me.'

'I hope not,' Megan said. 'I really hope not.'

'What about Duke's situation? His aunt?'

'Duke's injuries really frightened her. She's going to let him decide where he wants to live, or so she said. If he wants to stay here, I'd imagine she'd move back here. She isn't a bad person. She just thought she could make a life for him in Australia.'

'So she'd give up her life and move back just for Duke?'

Megan shrugged. 'They're family. What else could she do?'

This is all crazy, I thought, as we headed back on to the street. *Humans are nothing like we thought. They're like us. Just like us.*

16

We headed back to the old house to collect my things. As soon as we came around the corner, Megan stopped.

'Gardaí,' she said. 'Police.'

From where we stood, we could see the garda tape marking off the area as a crime scene.

'It's because of the gun,' Megan said. 'If it was just a random mugging, they wouldn't care, but the gun makes it something else. We can't go back inside. What did you leave there?'

'Just clothes. I have the important things here in my bag.'

'Let's go, then,' Megan said.

It took half an hour on the bus to get to Duke's grandmother's house. On the journey, I mulled over the new information about humans. Despite everything I'd heard, there was no doubt in my mind now that humans formed attachments. I had never once heard them talk about death. In fact, they acted as though death didn't exist. How strange, then, that on Terros, we talked about death all the time. People were so concerned about living for ever, about having an immune system that couldn't be breached, that death was all they thought about. I couldn't wait to tell Rio. I knew she would be fascinated.

I thought about Seb too.

Run, Dad had said. He must have known that Seb wanted to kill me. But why? What had I done to him? Sorrow nipped me deep inside. I knew how my parents would suffer, knowing I was at risk, but I was determined to get home. I wouldn't let Seb Roy destroy me.

Duke's house was in the middle of a small terrace. Trees lined the road and each dwelling had a small front garden with a metal gate. The grandmother opened the door. She was a tall thin woman, dressed in a dark green skirt and a soft white sweater, and she had her grey hair cut in a neat bob.

'You must be Aria,' she said. 'Please come in. Megan, my dear, will you join us?'

Megan shook her head. 'I'd better get back in time for lunch, but thank you, Mrs Simms. I might call by tomorrow.'

'Of course,' the older woman said. 'That would be lovely.'

And then we were alone.

'Let me show you to your room,' she said, striding ahead of me.

'Thank you so much for having me, Mrs … Mrs Simms.'

'Call me Grace, dear. I am happy to have you. Duke speaks very highly of you.'

'How is he?' I could hear the anxiety in my own voice.

'He is stable. They will operate tomorrow to set his jaw.'

'Is that a big operation?'

'Well –' Grace hesitated. 'They have to put in a plate, a metal plate, to stabilise it. That's what the surgeon told me.'

It sounded barbaric. On Terros, if such a thing happened, microscopic robots injected into the blood stream would repair the damage. It was relatively painless as a procedure and had no evil after-effects. I couldn't imagine cutting through flesh with a knife and inserting a metal plate. I shuddered. Grace put her arm about my shoulder.

'Don't worry,' she said. 'It sounds terrible but he is young and strong. The doctors say he'll be right as rain in a month or so. Come along, now. Your room is through here.'

It was a young girl's room – I saw that at once. A pink quilt cover and roses on the wallpaper.

'This was my daughter's room. Duke's mother.'

'I'm sorry,' I said. 'Duke told me that she ... that she had died.'

The old woman nodded. 'A car accident. A drunk driver ploughed into her. She had just bought a second-hand car. She was on her way here to show it to me.'

'That's terrible,' I said, and I meant it.

'It's life, I suppose. We all have to go some time. That was her time.'

'But she was so young.'

'It's not natural to bury your child,' Grace said. 'I should have gone first. Now, I look forward to seeing her on the other side.'

'Do you believe you will?'

'Of course. I couldn't go on if I didn't. Love doesn't end with death, you know. It gets stronger, if anything.' She smiled then, a sad smile, I thought. 'Hopefully my time is nearly up.'

'But ... you can't want to die?'

Grace laughed. 'I don't have much choice, do I? I've been here a long time. When you're as ancient as I am, there are things that are far worse than dying ... Being ill or helpless. That would be worse, wouldn't it? Being lonely. I have Duke. That keeps me going. Nearly all my family are long gone, all my friends. I have Carol, my daughter, who's home from Australia, and I have Duke. As long as they need me, I'll try to keep going.'

How brave she was! I didn't think I could face death like that. I was reminded of what Megan's father had said. *Keep on dancing.* It was good advice.

'And what about you?' Grace said now. 'Megan tells me that your father has been delayed abroad and you need somewhere to stay?'

I nodded. 'It's just for a few days. He'll come for me then and we'll go home together.'

'To London?'

'Yes.' *Please don't ask me anything about it.*

'I'll let you settle in. I'm heading back to the hospital soon to see Duke, but I'll leave some lunch for you in the fridge. You're vegetarian, Duke tells me.'

'Yes,' I said. 'Thank you.'

After Grace left, I tried to relax. The food that she'd left for me was a salad, full of bright fresh vegetables and nuts, but I didn't feel like eating. The old woman had unsettled me. She was so motherly.

The pain I felt when I thought of my own mother was visceral, holding me in a cruel vice. I needed to hear her voice. I took off my memory disc. Like most people on our planet, I didn't like handling it. It made me want to shiver, as though every nerve ending was exposed. I often thought that it should never be outside my body. It was too intimate, too dark.

I remembered the day my mum had given me the disc. I must have been about six. Mum and I were in the lab where Dad was working. Outside, the sun was in the east, shining through the delicate fabric of the work pod.

'Here it is, my darling! A brand new shiny disc,' she said.

How beautiful my mother looked, her long black hair tied back, her brown eyes deep and gentle.

She hung it carefully about my neck.

'What do I do now?'

My mother took my face between her hands. Cool smooth hands smelling of lilac.

'Just make happy memories little one. Make happy memories.'

'Why do we have a memory disc, Mum?'

126

'Because we live so long, Aria, thanks to the great work the lab does – we couldn't possibly carry all those memories with us throughout our lives. Or if we did, there wouldn't be enough room to learn new things. So, every so often, we upload our memories to our discs.'

'But what if a person didn't want to upload them? What if a person just wanted to keep them inside their own head?'

My mother stroked my hair.

'They might become ill, poppet. On the Shadow Planet – remember we talked about the Shadow last week?'

I nodded.

'On the Shadow they don't upload memory, and so, as they get older, they begin to lose their memories. It's an illness. In the end, they don't recognise their own children. You wouldn't want that to happen, would you?'

'But I don't have any children.'

My mother laughed then, a big warm sound that filled the room.

Warm tears flooded my eyes, even though I hadn't decided to cry. I had to get out of here. I needed to be back on my own planet. Determination surged through me, pumping adrenaline. I would go back. I would go home. I fingered my memory disc, and then I suddenly remembered the other disc. I rummaged in my bag until my fingers closed around cool metal. I pulled it out and looked at it. Seb's disc. I shuddered at the thought of handling it, not to mention putting it in my ear and delving into the mind of Seb Roy. But I knew that I had to do just that. I couldn't run away from this, pretend it wasn't happening, though I wanted to. My mind went back to the scene in the abandoned house. He said I was a mistake, *his mistake*, an experiment. Maybe there was something in his long-term memory that would give me a clue to what he was talking about.

Fifteen years ago I conducted an experiment. That's what he'd said. Would he have memories from that time on his disc? Or were they safely locked away in his head?

There was only one way to find out. I was surprised to see my hand tremble as I lifted the disc to my ear. I hesitated, for a second, like a bird about to take flight, then I smoothly inserted the disc.

I closed my eyes and said: *Fifteen years ago, an experiment that went wrong.* I repeated the words over and over again as Seb's memories flew by – ordinary days, work, food, play, repeated and repeated again. Seasons changing, day melting into night, night into day. Seb's world. My stomach lurched, and I felt as though I was being tossed about on the open sea. There was a darkness about Seb's memories, a feeling of cold and a taste of bitterness. I wanted to haul the cursed disc out of my ear and to throw it as far away from me as I could, but I gritted my teeth and waited for the showreel to slow down. And it did.

Seb was younger, but it was undeniably Seb, and he was here on Earth. I closed my eyes and focused.

Seb was walking across a park, taking long strides, head down, shoulders hunched. I thought I recognised the park. Where had I seen it before? I tried to focus on the 'film' in front of me. He is through the park now, moving out through the tall black gates, passing a crowd of students laughing and jostling one another in grey and blue school uniforms. He walks to the traffic lights and presses the button, crosses and goes left. He doesn't look up at the streetname, though I wish he would. This is somewhere he knows: he doesn't need to check the name. There are houses lining the street. Now he's stopping. He looks up and down the street quickly and goes through a blue door. There is a sign but I can't read it.

The memory jumps then. It's later, Seb is inside the house now, it seems, and there is a woman. She stands in a window, her hands folded protectively over her swollen, pregnant stomach. The window is old-fashioned, arched, and she is dwarfed by it. She is tall and she's slim apart from her stomach, with dark skin that glows with health. Her hair is a mass of small tight plaits decorated with coloured beads. She is wearing brown trousers and a silky green shirt. I feel what Seb feels. It's a warm feeling that doesn't seem like Seb any more. There's softness there, and something else, something fragile. He leans forward and kisses the woman. I feel her lips, warm and soft, and the memory ends.

I removed the disc. I sat for a while trying to piece things together. Seb had been here on Earth as a young man, and he had known a human woman, loved her even. She was pregnant. Was Seb the baby's father? My mind didn't want to accept that. How could someone from Terros contemplate having a baby with a human woman? A woman from the Shadow Planet? And why would Seb Roy do that? Maybe it *wasn't* his baby. He'd said he'd conducted an experiment. I was sure now that this woman was part of that – as I was. But how did I fit in to his story, if it all happened on Earth? I had never been to Earth until now.

I felt restless and knew I wouldn't relax until I got some answers. I stood up, not sure where I would go, and then suddenly something clicked. The park! The park Seb had walked across when he went to see the woman. I knew it. It was the park I had gone to the day I first saw Seb. My heart galloped. It wasn't much, but it was a start. If I could find the house, maybe the woman would still be there, maybe she could help me to work out what Seb's experiment had been about.

I grabbed my coat and went back outdoors and straight to the bus stop. Why was everything so slow on Earth? I got on the bus and watched the streets change from leafy house-lined places to the busier centre where the park was. We rounded a corner and

I saw the tall black iron gates, exactly as they had been on Seb's memory disc. I got off the bus and tried to take the exact same route as I had seen Seb take. I went from the gates to the traffic lights and turned left. The street was as I remembered, lined with rather tall, old houses, but no blue door.

Why would there be? Seb had been young in the memory, so it could be ten, fifteen years ago. This was pointless! I would never find the house. I looked up again, and this time something caught my eye. One of the buildings had a tall arched window on the first floor. Hadn't he remembered the woman standing in a window that looked like that? I headed straight for the building. I stood outside the door looking at the panel of bells, each with a number beside it. I had no idea what to do next, when the door opened and a young man walked out.

'Going in?' he said.

He didn't have to ask me twice. I raced up the stairs and stopped on the first-floor landing. Apartment 3. I knocked, and after a minute the door opened and a small old man stood there.

'Yes?' he said.

'I'm sorry,' I said. 'I'm looking for an old friend of my parents. She used to live here. A black woman?'

The man shook his head.

'I've lived here for fourteen years,' he said. 'I don't know who had the place before that. I'm sorry. I can't help you. Do you know her name?'

I shook my head. Whatever little hope I had was slowly melting away.

'No,' I said. 'I don't.'

The old man nodded.

'You could try Connie Burke,' he said. She lives upstairs in number 5. She's been here a long time. She might remember.'

He closed the door and I made for the stairs again. I didn't stop until I got to number 5.

Connie Burke was ancient and time had made her face sag and her hair turn grey. She didn't answer at first when I asked her about the black woman and I thought it was another waste of time, but then she looked at me and said: 'Kanise. Poor Kanise Lee. She used to live there. A nice wee girl with a beautiful smile.'

'Where is she now?' I asked. 'Do you know where she lives?'

Connie shook her head. 'She is living with the Lord Most High,' she said. 'Died in childbirth. She left here in an ambulance in the dead of night and never came back. I asked the landlord about her and he told me. Poor, poor girl. I never heard another thing about her, though I would have gone to her funeral. I don't even know if the child lived. Kanise's family were in Jamaica. Maybe they took it home with them. I hope so. I hope it lived.'

17

ack in Grace's house, I looked again at the salad that she had left for me. I should eat, but I had no appetite. I dreaded putting Seb's disc back in my ear, but my curiosity was killing me. I had to know what happened. *Don't think about it*, I told myself. *Just do it*. I lay on the sofa and inserted the disc.

Seb is in a hospital, standing by a bed. Kanise is lying there, her skin grey and covered with a sheen of sweat. I could feel Seb's fear.

'The baby?' Kanise says, her voice hoarse and weak, barely audible.

'They took it … her … away,' Seb says. 'She was cold.'

'You have to take care of her,' Kanise says, and there is an urgency in her voice. 'Take her home with you. Promise me, Seb.'

Seb nods.

'Say it,' Kanise says. 'Please, say it.'

'I will take care of her,' Seb says, though his voice sounds strangled. 'I'll take her home with me, but please, Kanise … please …'

Kanise sighs and closes her eyes. For a second, Seb just stands there, and then a nurse touches his shoulder.

'She's gone,' she says. 'I'm sorry.'

The pain was so violent I could hardly bear it – Seb's pain – raw and stabbing. He falls to his knees beside the bed.

I had to take the disc out. I couldn't breathe. I didn't know anyone could feel pain as sharp as that, as deep as that. It was horrible. Kanise had died. Seb had been heartbroken. But what about the baby? Could he have taken it back to Terros?

I was so exhausted from the whole experience that I fell into a deep sleep. My dreams were full of frightening images: Seb, a gun, an enormous pigeon, my father being chased through the streets, a man dying on the DART, a small baby struggling to take a breath and me falling, falling through the stars, and on to a swirling blue planet. When I ran out of dreams, I woke up.

I was shivering. I felt my forehead. Hot. And yet my hands and feet were freezing. Raised temperature, my brain told me, but my body didn't seem to be able to do anything about it. I tried to sit up, but I didn't have the strength. My bones ached and my mouth felt dry. I had to get help. Was this the virus, or something else? I didn't know how my immune system would react. Would I die? I didn't want to die, not here, all alone.

A shrill sound startled me. A bell. The telephone. I could see it on the small table in the far corner of the room, beside a framed photograph of Grace and Duke. If I could only get to it, maybe someone would come – I mightn't have to die.

I let my body fall on to the floor and started to crawl. I could feel the nylon fibres of the carpet beneath my fingers. I pushed myself forward. Please don't stop ringing till I get there. Please. A few more feet. It was still ringing. I reached the leg of the table. I stretched up. The phone stopped ringing. *No!* I collapsed onto the ground. Sweat poured down my face, stinging my eyes. *Can't sleep*, I told myself. *Have to keep going.* I pulled myself on to my hands and knees again, and as I did, the phone rang. This time I didn't hesitate. I clambered up and grabbed the receiver. There was a green button. I pressed it.

'Hello?'

Relief shot through me.

'Megan!'

'Listen, Aria. I'm at the hospital. Duke has got some kind of infection. Grace is going to stay the night here, with Carol. I'm coming over to stay with you.'

'Megan!' I said again.

'Is there something wrong?'

'Yes,' I managed to say, before the phone fell from my hand. I lay on the ground, the carpet soft beneath my cheek. I could hear Megan calling me.

'Aria? Aria! Answer me.'

It didn't matter. I had to close my eyes. There were worse things than dying.

It was to be the longest night in my life. When Megan arrived I was barely conscious, though I did manage to come round and let her help me up the stairs to bed. All the time, my head thrummed and my eyes felt like they were being pierced by needles.

I fell asleep then, and when I woke, Megan was still there.

'We have to go to the hospital,' she said.

That was enough to make me wake up and pay attention.

'No,' I said. 'I can't …'

'No matter how bad things get, Aria, at least you'll be alive.'

'You … don't … understand,' I said. It was so hard to get the words out.

'Close curtains,' I said with my next breath.

'Are your eyes hurting?'

'No. Pigeons.'

'Pigeons?'

'Phobia.'

Megan closed the curtains.

'You're so pale, Aria. I should call an ambulance. Please let me. I'll protect you. I promise. Just rest. I'll go downstairs and call –'

Panic bloomed, filling my stomach, my throat. Overwhelming panic. *Tell her! The time has come.*

'Please, Aria. You need an ambulance.' Megan's voice had a note of desperation.

'Cut me!'

The words were out now. They couldn't be taken back.

'What? Are you mad?'

'If … you want to know the truth, cut me. Just a pinprick. You'll see.'

Megan frowned. 'What will I see?'

'Please. You'll understand then.'

Megan opened her bag and took out a small nail scissors.

'Are you sure about this?'

'Please.'

A tiny sting. Then I could feel the blood. I looked at Megan's face. All the colour had drained from it.

'It's blue. Your blood is bright blue.'

'Yes.'

Megan took a step backwards. 'What's the matter with you? What does it mean? Is it the virus? How could it do that to you?'

'It's nothing to do with the virus.'

'It isn't? Well, what is it then? How can you have blue blood?'

'It means … it means … that I'm not fully … not entirely … human.'

'Not human? Is this a joke?'

'No joke. I'm not from Earth.'

I found myself watching her as though from a distance. I saw the emotional trauma on Megan's face.

'Not from … where are you from, then?'

Here goes.

'I am from a planet called Terros. In another galaxy. A long way from here.'

'You're delirious.'

Megan was beside me again, putting a wet compress on my head. I took her hand and removed it, firmly.

'No, Megan. I'm not delirious. It's true.'

Megan looked frightened now. She dropped my hand. 'You're telling me that you are … you're … an alien?'

'I am.'

'And your father?'

'Yes.'

'If you are … from another planet, what are you doing here? Why the attack on the DART?'

I sighed. I was too tired. I couldn't go into it now.

'Need sleep,' I managed before disappearing into my own head.

When I awoke again, it was still dark. Megan was asleep on a chair beside the bed. I sat up. I felt better. A lot better. My immune system had kicked in. I was sure of it.

'You're awake.' Megan's voice startled me.

'I feel better,' I said.

'Are you still an alien?'

'I'm sorry about that, Megan. I would never have told you if you hadn't mentioned the hospital. I couldn't go there. You know what would have happened.'

'*E.T.*'

'Sorry?'

'It's a film about an alien.'

'I'm sorry. I don't know about human films.'

'I don't know much about aliens.'

'But you believe me?'

'I don't know that I do. One minute you're a terrorist from London – now you're an alien from Mars.'

'Not from Mars. There's no life on Mars. I'm from Terros, beside the Seven Sisters. It's in another galaxy.'

'I was being sarcastic.'

'Sorry.'

I had no idea how to deal with this girl. How could I make her understand?

'So this planet, Terros, why do you want to kill us?'

'We don't.' I was lying again, but I had no choice.

'But your father ...'

'My father was testing a strain of the flu virus.'

'On us? Why?'

'You are our Shadow Planet. Lots of planets have them.'

'Lots of planets? You are not the only other planet that has life on it?'

'Of course not.'

'What do you mean we are a Shadow Planet?'

'A Shadow Planet is a planet that exists to service another planet.'

'Service?'

'We do medical research, for example. Sociological studies. Agricultural experiments.'

Megan stood up. Her cheeks were red. 'And what gives you the right ... to ... use ... us like that?'

'I don't know. I was brought up to believe that it didn't matter, because you didn't form attachments. It didn't matter because you all die.'

'Do you not die?'

'Not normally. We have put all of our resources into our immune systems. We don't succumb to disease.'

'But *you* did? You did succumb?'

'Yes. I did.'

I could see Megan desperately trying to process all of the information that was hurtling towards her.

'Are there … are there … many of you here?'

'No. We don't need to be here most of the time. We get the data through pigeons.'

'Excuse me? Pigeons?'

'They act like spies. No-one here ever notices them.'

'That's why you wanted me to pull the curtains.'

'Yes.'

'You'd better be telling me the truth.'

'I am.'

'Like you were when you told me you were from London?'

'I didn't want you to know who I really was. I admit it. But I'm telling you the truth now.'

Sort of.

'And you thought we didn't form attachments?'

'There was evidence to suggest it.'

'Really?'

'Humans do a lot of bad things to one another.'

I could see Megan was getting angry again.

'Have you seen how my mother, my brother and I love one another?'

'Yes.'

'Humans also do good things.'

'Of course.'

'And you just go round colonising other planets?'

'We don't colonise other planets. We didn't colonise you. We created you.'

138

18

Megan's face was as white as milk. *She's in shock,* I told myself. Meanwhile, I was feeling stronger with every passing minute.

'We are only one thousand years old?'

'Yes,' I said.

'You said that you do medical experiments. Do you have cancer on your planet?'

'No. The gene for cancer would have been neutralised before birth.'

'But you don't share that technology with us?'

I could see where this was going. 'We share some knowledge with you. We gave you a vaccine for TB.'

'Really? And how long did you make us wait for that? How many of us died before you put a stop to it?'

'I'm sorry. You are our Shadow Planet.'

'How dare you? How dare you call us that!'

'I'm sorry, Megan. I'm fourteen years old. I don't have all the answers.'

'You're sorry? That's a joke. You come here to experiment on us. You let us die, though you could stop it. You let us suffer because you won't tell us what you know – and you're sorry?'

Megan was on her feet, grabbing her coat.

'And I tried to help you. You make me sick. How can you look at yourself in the mirror? How?'

I could see the tears welling up in her eyes.

'Megan …' I began, but Megan was already moving. Seconds later, I heard the front door slam, and she was gone.

The loneliness was like a thick blanket descending on me. Megan had been my friend; now I didn't have her. She had every right to be angry. We had behaved shamefully. I decided to cry. As small children on Terros, we'd been taught to cry when we felt overwhelmed or stressed.

I sat on the floor and bowed my head. Tears flowed freely down my cheeks. My nose clogged up. My throat ached. As I cried, I felt the tension leave my muscles. Twenty minutes later, I gulped in air, my body shuddered and I stopped. I wiped my nose on my sleeve and used my skirt to mop my eyes. I was exhausted. I didn't cry very often, but I knew the benefits. Crying lowers blood pressure and pulse rate, it eliminates toxins and harmful stress hormones, raises levels of serotonin and reduces stress.

I was so lost in my own thoughts that I almost missed the sound of the door closing downstairs. I sat upright. Who was it? Megan?

'Aria!'

It was Duke's grandmother. I ran down the stairs to meet her.

'How's Duke?' I said, as I stepped into the hall.

The old face tightened.

'Not too well, my dear,' she said. 'Not well at all, in fact.'

'Oh, no. What's happened?'

'It's the infection. It's … it's out of control. He has a thing called … septicaemia.'

'But they have antibiotics in that hospital, don't they?'

The old woman put an arm around my shoulders and pulled me close. 'They do. But they aren't working. There's nothing they can do now but wait.'

140

I pulled away from Grace's embrace.

'Wait? Wait for what?'

'Come into the kitchen with me, Aria. My old legs aren't too good with all this standing.'

We walked into the kitchen. It was then I noticed how pale and drawn Duke's grandmother was. Exhausted.

'Sit down,' I said. 'I'll make you tea.'

I'd seen it being made. I knew how to do it. *Boil water.*

'He may not survive, Aria.'

Put tea in pot. Three spoons.

'The doctor said that hope is now fading. If this new drug doesn't work …'

Pour the boiling water on the tea.

'I just wish I could swap places with him. I would happily go now, but he has his whole life ahead of him.'

'Sugar?' I said. 'Milk?'

'Both, thank you. Have you eaten?' Grace said.

I tried not to think about food. I was sure I would be ill if I ate any. I shook my head. 'Not hungry.'

I poured the tea carefully. Two cups. Grace took one, and I sat beside her at the table. I cradled the hot cup.

'We have to face this, Aria. We may lose him. I don't want you to get a shock. You need to prepare yourself.'

I had once had a bad infection, one of my famous glitches. I had had blood poisoning. How had they cured it? I had no idea. I was only seven or eight at the time. But my memories would be on my disc.

'Excuse me,' I said. 'I'll be back.'

This time I took the stairs two at a time. In the bedroom, I closed the door and lay on the bed. Carefully, I extracted the disc from where it lay nestled in the hollow on my chest. I slipped it into my ear. *Illness. Unwell.* I used the trigger words to bring me to the right place. And then I found it.

It is night time. I am in bed. I wake feeling hot. My head is on fire and my limbs ache. Is my bodysuit not working? I have to get help. But I can't sit up. I try, but it hurts too much. My head hurts when I try to lift it. I cry out. The effort makes my head hurt even more. Hot tears flow down my face, under my chin, on to my chest.

'Mum!' I manage to get the word out.

Movement. Light. My mother's voice.

'It's all right, darling.'

Cool hand on my forehead. The smell of lilac.

'Lucas!' Her voice sounding urgent.

'I'm here, Aria. Dad is here.'

Then nightmares and nausea. I feel myself being moved, but I can't open my eyes. We are in the transport hub. I force one eye to open. My parents hover above me, frowning.

'We can't tell anyone, Lucas.' My mother, voice tense and hushed.

'Don't worry. Seb will know what to do. I've just alerted him. He'll see her at his own laboratory.'

'Can we trust him?'

My father pauses. 'We have to.'

I am in Seb's laboratory now. Big lights over my head. Someone calling out numbers. My father.

'Blood pressure eighty over one hundred, falling.'

'Pulse thready.'

'White blood cell count ...'

'Try carapemine. Two hundred mills.'

'Carapemine delivered.'

'What else have we given her?'

'Broad-spectrum antibiotics.'

142

'No use on their own. They need to be combined with an anti-inflammatory. Try dersisolone.'

The picture blurs. My mother calling out numbers. Dosage amounts. Seb's voice. My father's voice.

'Three doses? Isn't that a lot?'

'That's the point! Get on with it. And more fluids. Drip wide open …'

'Blood pressure responding.'

And then my mother's voice. 'Oh, Lucas! How did this happen?'

Reluctantly, I took out the disc. It was strange to see that scene again – the night of the first fever. I shook myself. I had to write the information down. Fluids. Carapemine. Broad-spectrum antibiotics and dersisolone. I wrote down the exact dosages.

I ran back to Duke's grandmother. The old woman was still sitting on the chair where I left her, but now she had her mobile phone in her hand and was staring at the screen.

'What is it?' I asked.

'His blood pressure is dropping. My daughter is sending a car for me.'

'Take me with you.'

'No, Aria. It's no place for a child.'

'I can help him.'

'I don't think so, Aria,' Grace said, pulling on her coat. 'No-one can help him now.'

'You know I told you that my father is a doctor?'

'Yes.'

'He texted me. Told me what Duke needs. He's done a lot of research into septicaemia.'

I saw something like hope flit across Grace's face. A car hooted outside.

'Come on, then,' she said. 'We need to hurry.'

143

19

The hospital was antiquated. People lay on trolleys in the corridor of the emergency wing. Oxygen tanks, masks, drips and people – especially people – everywhere. People coughing and sneezing. People talking and touching. It was like something from a nightmare.

We hurried through the packed corridors and took the lift to the second floor.

'This way,' Grace said.

We stopped outside a small room. *Nil by mouth* the sign on the door said.

Duke was lying on a large white bed. A young woman sat on a chair beside him. I guessed that she was the aunt. He had a drip in his right arm and his chest was littered with cables, all of which fed into a monitor beside him. It looked as if a giant octopus had sat on his chest. His face was grey. His eyes were closed. His hands lay still on the starched sheet.

The young woman looked up, her eyes full of tears. She shook her head. I wasn't sure what that meant.

'This is Aria,' Grace said. 'Her father is a doctor. He's investigated this condition and he has sent a remedy. Who can we talk to?'

'A remedy?' the woman said, standing. 'There is no remedy. His organs are starting to shut down.'

'Who can we talk to?'

'Mother …'

'We are wasting time. Aria's father may be able to help. What have we got to lose?'

Only Duke, I thought. *Only Duke.*

'The nurse is next door. Maybe she could …'

Grace didn't wait. I followed her to the desk in the room next door.

'I am Duke's grandmother.'

'I remember you,' the nurse said.

'We need to speak to the consultant.'

The nurse frowned. 'Is it something I can help with?'

'No!' Grace's voice was as sharp as a tack. 'Get the consultant.'

The nurse picked up the phone. Ten minutes later we had explained all to the kindly Asian woman who stood in front of us. She looked again at my notes.

'Can I speak to your father?'

'There isn't time,' I said. 'He said that you have to act at once. It may already be too late.'

The woman frowned. She looked again at the piece of paper I had given her. 'I'm sorry,' she said. 'But apart from the antibiotics, I've never heard of any of these drugs.'

My heart plummeted. How could I have been so stupid? These were Terros drugs, made with technology that was light years ahead of these people. I felt Grace sag beside me as if all the air had suddenly left her.

'Can you get Carol for me, dear?' she said.

I hurried away and let myself into Duke's room, where Carol was still sitting by his bed. 'I think Grace needs you,' I said.

She jumped up and went through the door. I sat by Duke's bed and took his hand in mine. It was cold, heavy, lifeless. I could see that the life force was leaving him. He was too young to die.

He deserved a second chance. And then it struck me like a thunderbolt. A second chance! The pill. I still had it stashed inside my memory-disc locket. I grabbed the chain from around my neck and took out the pill.

Would it work on a human? Would it kill him? He was going to die anyway. It had to be worth a shot. But what about me? This was my safety net, the only thing standing between me and death. I might need it. I looked at Duke again. None of this was his fault – and he was dying *now*. I might only be a girl who had fallen from the skies, but I wasn't going to leave things worse than I had found them. This was something I could do.

Nil by mouth, I thought with a shrug. Gently, I prised Duke's lips open and slipped the tiny pill into his mouth. I knew that it would dissolve instantly. Now all I had to do was wait.

The door opened and the consultant came back in, followed by Grace and Carol. I couldn't bear to look at them, but I could feel their grief. I stared at Duke, looking for any sign of recovery, but there was nothing.

The consultant checked the monitor. Grace took my hand and squeezed it. I looked at Duke. Still nothing. It hadn't worked. The consultant checked his pulse and shook her head.

'I'm sorry.'

'Give him time,' I said, trying to keep the panic out of my voice. What if I'd killed him? I tried to swallow the lump that had formed in my throat.

And then, without warning, his body jerked. A convulsion? The consultant tensed.

'Wait!' she said. 'Duke?'

All eyes focused on the boy in the bed. His eyelids fluttered. He opened his mouth and sucked in air. Then his eyes opened. He muttered something.

Suddenly, everything speeded up. Nurses came in. Another doctor. The consultant listened to his chest, took his pulse. Tubes were pulled out, others put in.

The consultant turned, her face lit up with a smile.

'He's doing much better,' she said. 'He will probably sleep now for a while.'

Relief flooded my body, followed by joy. I hadn't killed him. He would live. I sat with his aunt and grandmother for another hour. Nurses and doctors came and went, and even though they wouldn't promise anything, all agreed that he was much better.

'Why don't you two go for some tea?' I said. 'I'll sit with him for a while.'

Duke's grandmother shook her head.

But Carol said: 'Aria is right, mother. We could do with a cup of tea.'

As the door closed behind them, my head was raging with new thoughts, new ideas. This wasn't right. Terros was using these poor people to make themselves stronger. People like Duke. I knew that my own people genuinely believed that humans didn't form attachments, didn't feel pain in the same way as the people of Terros, but I now knew that wasn't true. Maybe we just wanted to believe that? Was it something that parliament had come up with to stop us from questioning their methods? I was certain of one thing: now that I knew the truth, I could never accept what was going on.

Duke stirred and then slowly opened his eyes. 'Aria,' he said.

'Hush,' I said. 'Don't talk. You've been very unwell.'

He managed a weak smile.

'Good to see you.'

He closed his eyes again. I didn't want him to die, not now, not ever. I wanted him to live without the fear of dying, just like I did.

I wanted him to run and laugh and dance. As I sat by Duke's bed, I remembered what Megan had told me about her dad. I whispered in his ear: 'Keep dancing, Duke.'

I didn't hear the door open.

'You?! What are you doing here?'

Megan.

'I ... I came to see Duke,' I said.

Megan glared at me.

'To gather data, I suppose. What? Not enough pigeons about?'

I could hear the anger in her voice, a rage twisting her words, and I could see it in her face, in her steely eyes and in the curl of her lip.

'I only wanted to ... I wanted to ...'

The door opened again. A nurse came in.

'So this is our miracle boy?'

She took Duke's wrist and smiled at me.

'I've never seen anything like it. We were sure he was gone.'

When the nurse left, Megan turned to me.

'You had something to do with it, didn't you?' she said.

I didn't answer. I didn't want her praise. I didn't deserve it. Everything that had happened to Duke was my fault.

She took a step towards me.

'So could you cure everyone in this hospital? If you wanted to?'

I saw the bewilderment in her face.

'No. Of course not,' I said. 'I used something – a once-off thing. A kind of safety net I had.'

Megan shook her head, anger bubbling up in her eyes again. 'I still don't know what you are. Are you even telling the truth? Prove to me that you are an alien.'

'You saw my blood. It's not like yours.'

She frowned.

'That could be a trick. Show me something else.'

I couldn't imagine why she thought I'd want to trick her into believing I was an alien, but I had definitely lied to her, so I racked my brain. What could I show her to make her believe me? Unconsciously, my hand went to my memory disc.

I hesitated. The thought of it was repulsive, but if I let Megan in for a minute, just one minute, surely then she would believe.

With shaking hands, I removed my disc. Megan looked at me suspiciously, her green eyes scanning my face.

'What's that?'

'It's my memory disc. Unlike you, we don't carry memory with us all of the time. On this disc, you'll be able to access most of my memories since I was about seven years old.'

'Really?'

'Yes. It's like watching a film. And you have to understand, this is difficult for me. You can only look for a minute. OK?'

'OK.'

I took the disc and placed it in Megan's ear. Megan closed her eyes. I couldn't watch. I turned away and gazed out the window at the people coming and going below me. A warm sun bathed my face. I tried not to think about what was happening behind me. Megan was in my head, going through my thoughts, my feelings. She was inside my skin. Shame flooded through me. What would she think of me? Would she sense all my weaknesses, my pride, my stupid hopes?

A minute later Megan tapped me on the shoulder.

'That's wild,' she said. 'I was in your head. I was on your planet, looking at three moons, and your mother …'

I held up my hand. 'Please,' I said, 'don't talk about it.'

I replaced the disc.

'I still don't know what to think,' Megan said, but her voice was soft. 'You really are an alien. And you really are here to harm us. I can't get past that.'

'You're not wrong,' I said. 'We're here to experiment on you, to use you, and yes, even hurt you. My people don't believe that you feel things like we do. They don't believe that you form attachments.'

Megan shook her head. 'How could they think that? Why?'

'You die, Megan. We don't. You die after a really short time. And you know you will die. My people didn't believe that you would attach under those circumstances.'

Megan was silent for a beat. Then: 'And now? What do you believe now?'

'We were wrong. I used to be so proud of our planet and the work we did, but now … I want to make it right.'

'Really? Can you do that?'

'I don't know, but I can try. I can try, if I can contact my people, get home.' Desperation bubbled up inside me. 'But I'm trapped here. I have no way of getting home. And that's not all. There is a man from home, Seb Roy. He's the one who hurt Duke. He wants to hurt me too and my parents. I need your help, Megan. I can't let him find me.'

I searched Megan's face for a reaction. It was difficult to know what she was thinking.

'What do you want me to do?' she said.

'I'm not sure yet. I've been so preoccupied with Duke. But I have to get back home somehow.'

'How did you get here?'

'In a star-ship, but Dad will have taken that to get home in.'

'But this other bloke, Seb, he must have had a ship too, mustn't he?'

Why had that not occurred to me? Megan was right. Seb's star-ship had to be here somewhere. My mind was racing. 'And he would have landed at Rossport, where we landed.'

'So we go to Rossport and find it,' Megan said.

'But … I can't … I can't pilot it. I don't know how.'

The door opened suddenly. There were two police officers in uniform, one male, one female – and the social worker.

'That's her,' the social worker said.

Megan jumped to her feet.

'What's going on? What do you want with her?'

The policewoman stepped forward.

'You are Aria Riga?'

'Yes.'

'Aria Riga, you are under arrest as a suspect in the terrorist attack on the DART to Bray on Thursday, the twenty-sixth of October. You do not have to say anything …'

I was so consumed by conflicting emotions – fear, anger, disbelief – that I hardly heard her. Huge feelings and no way to filter them, no way to control them. I looked at Megan. She was pale and stunned, didn't catch my eye. The policeman stepped forward and snapped handcuffs onto my wrists, the metal, harsh and cold, pressing against my skin.

For a second all was quiet. The only sound in the room was the cooing of a pigeon balanced on the window ledge.

20

The questioning was insistent. The room was small and airless. The social worker sat beside me, in lieu of my guardian. My mind was in lockdown. My whole body was relaxed and I was concentrating on my mantra: *Silence.* I repeated the word over and over. It conjured up images of peaceful fields peppered with wild flowers, small streams tumbling over rocks, the three moons suspended in the night sky. The voices droned on. Two detectives sat opposite, a stout man with glasses and a small wiry woman.

Soft voice.

Loud voice.

Desk bang.

Chair fall.

It was all happening far away. Far from the stream and the flowers.

Bang!

Another hand slamming on the desk.

Trickle, trickle, the stream falling over the rocks.

Bang!

A door slammed.

Silence.

The social worker touched my arm. I opened my eyes. The police were gone. Slowly, I brought everything into focus. The tacky yellow-topped table, the harsh white light, the stained grey walls.

'I don't think you're handling this very well, Aria,' the social worker said, her lips pursed as though trying to hold back her words. 'They won't stop until you tell them the truth.'

'What truth? I know nothing about the attack.'

'The police believe that your father carried out the attack.'

'And I am to blame for that?'

'Of course not, but if you're innocent you have no reason not to speak to the police.'

'I am innocent.'

'Well, then,' the social worker said, 'just tell the guards what happened, or better still write it down.'

I thought it over. I needed to give them something, a story, something they could believe. I would write it. That might be safer. I asked the social worker for paper and a pen. She smiled.

Minutes later, I composed my tale. I knew nothing of India. I hadn't been there since I was a baby. We had been living in London. My father brought me to Dublin on a business trip. Then, he disappeared. I had not heard from him.

I didn't know what the police had made of my statement. I just knew they were letting me leave the airless room. They would have to run background checks to confirm the validity of my story, they said, but that would take time.

'You are going to stay with a foster family until this is sorted.' The social worker seemed pleased with that arrangement. 'You're lucky they didn't put you in a remand home. Very lucky.'

I didn't feel lucky. I felt as though something had broken inside of me. My whole life was coming undone, spiralling helplessly, getting more and more complicated. I wanted to go home. I wanted my parents. I wanted Rio. I wanted to be amongst people who were like me, who knew me and who didn't find me alien. I just wanted it all to stop.

But it wouldn't stop. Soon, I was in a car on my way to the Duggan family. The social worker twittered on about how nice they were. They were a retired couple. No children. But they were very experienced. They would sort out a school for me, get me back on an even keel. I listened, but inside I was numb.

The Duggans lived in a terraced house in a small estate. Mrs Duggan, Rose, was a large woman with short grey hair and two wide blue eyes. When she smiled, I saw that her two front teeth were smeared with pink lipstick. Mr Duggan was smaller, with thin lips and a smell of tobacco. They showed me to my bedroom and I collapsed on the bed as soon as they closed the door. The room was tiny, the walls covered in bumpy paper painted a sick shade of yellow.

I wanted my father. The yearning was like a small animal gnawing on my insides. But I also wanted to go home and tell people the truth, tell them that my father was a patriot. He would never betray Terros. Seb had told him that our mission was top secret so my father wouldn't have discussed it with anyone. He would have assumed that Seb was passing on orders received from parliament. He would have had no way of knowing that Seb was on a solo run. My poor father! I had a lump in my throat thinking about him. He had looked up to Seb – the brilliant scientist and his friend. I had to let people on Terros know that my father was innocent. I had to. And I needed to do it before Seb Roy became leader of Terros.

Outside, the wind was rising and rain pelted the window. The police – the guards – would be back with more questions. The social worker would watch my every move. And Seb Roy was still out there. I fingered the disc about my neck, now two discs. I took out the one belonging to Seb. I had to find out how his story ended. I held it in my hand for a second, then slipped it into my ear.

Seb is still on the Shadow Planet, but now he is holding a baby. It must be Kanise's child, but what Seb is feeling is something akin to hatred. He puts the baby down and picks up a syringe. He injects something into the child's arm and she falls asleep.

The memory jumps then and it's later. Seb is on Terros in the Blue Laboratory. All about him are babies at various stages of development in their plastic wombs. A nurse comes in.

'The parents are here, Seb,' she says in a bright voice.

'I'm on my way,' he says.

In the reception area, a couple is waiting for him. My heart skips a beat. It's my parents – Mum and Dad – and Mum is holding a baby. Is that *me*? Could that be me?

'Congratulations!' Seb says. 'She's a perfect specimen. A healthy baby girl. She doesn't come with a manual, but any problems, come straight back to me. I am her designated physician.'

It *is* me. I am that tiny baby. Kanise's child.

Seb's child.

I feel like I have fallen down an elevator shaft. I can barely breathe, but the action continues. My parents laugh, but I can feel the tension in Seb Roy. That tension floods my body, his tension, his angst. It almost knocks me out. Inside, he's screaming.

Get her out of my sight! Go! Take her!

That's what he wants to say but he can't. He has to keep up the pretence just until they are out of the building. As soon as they leave – as soon as we leave – he drops all pretence, pain like I have never felt courses through him – through me, as I experience his memory – sadness, grief, rage.

I pulled the disc out of my ear. I lay there for a long time, numb, paralysed by my own thoughts. *I am Seb and Kanise's daughter. That is why I have human DNA – the maternal DNA is dominant. Mum and Dad are not my parents.* It felt like someone had split open the ground beneath my feet, and I was falling. *Seb Roy is my father and my mother is a stranger. Seb Roy! How could that be? I don't even like him. Why would he do that? Why would he smuggle me on to Terros and then disown me?* The rejection felt like a sting. I didn't want him to be my father, but it hurt that he didn't want me.

I had tea with the Duggans. A meal of beans and chips and sliced white bread that tasted like plastic. They ate it with big mugs of sweet, strong tea. Throughout the meal they tried to talk to me.

Missing home are you?

Don't get chips like this where you come from.

Heard anything from your dad?

Religious is he?

And all the time their narrowed eyes watched me, hoping for a titbit. And that became the pattern of my days. Seven days of breakfast and dinner and tea. Seven days of cocoa and television that I didn't want to watch. Seven days of misery. And all the while Seb's story was playing and replaying in my mind. On the eighth day, I was lying on my bed trying to relax when Mrs Duggan knocked on the door.

'A visitor for you,' she said.

I sat up abruptly.

'Who?'

'Come down and see. I'm not your secretary!'

It was Megan. We sat at the kitchen table with Mrs Duggan hovering. I could see her straining to hear every word and so very few words passed between us.

I asked about Duke.

'Better,' Megan said. 'He's home from hospital.'

And then the sound of a phone ringing. Mrs Duggan pulled out her mobile phone and scuttled out to the hall to answer it.

'I have to get out of here,' I said as soon as the door closed.

'And where would you go?'

'Well, to Rossport,' I said. 'I have to get there so that I can get home. Seb must have landed there too, and that is where his star-ship will be.'

'But how will you get away from here?'

I frowned.

'She goes to bingo on Saturday night. He stays in watching television, which makes him sleepy. I could try then.'

'Go to the supermarket over the road. Out the door and turn right. It's just beyond the lights. I'll meet you there at nine on Saturday. OK?'

'Sure. And, Megan … thank you.'

Mrs Duggan came in again.

'I'd better go,' Megan said, standing up.

'Maybe you can call in again next week?' I said.

'Does your mother know where you are?' Mrs Duggan interjected. 'I wouldn't be making plans. Aria has a lot of fences to climb before she can be lolling around with her friends.'

And you are enjoying every minute of my misfortune, I thought. I didn't understand the malice in the woman, but I could almost smell it.

After Megan left, I worked on my escape plan. It all hinged on Mr Duggan falling asleep in front of the television. I watched him each night, and each night the flickering light of the box eventually knocked him out. My confidence grew.

On Saturday morning, I was relieved when Mrs Duggan commented on the bingo night.

'Maude is calling for me tonight at half seven,' she told her husband.

'That's good,' he said, between mouthfuls of porridge.

I relaxed. All was going to plan.

'That social worker is going to call by,' Mrs Duggan continued.

'Tonight?' I said, my heart plummeting.

'How would I know?' Mrs Duggan said. 'She doesn't confide in me.'

'But she must have mentioned a time?'

'Must she now? Well I have news for you. She didn't.'

Mr Duggan laughed. 'Not like you have a hectic schedule, luveen! You'll be here whenever she calls.'

'Can I call her?' I asked. 'Just to check?'

Mrs Duggan picked up the empty plates. 'She has more to do than chatting to the like of you! She'll come when she comes. Clear that table now and get about your business. Call her indeed!'

I stood up. I cleared the table and went back to my room.

21

The day pushed on. No sign of the social worker. As soon as Mr Duggan fell asleep, I would take my bag and slip out the back door and around to the front of the house, keeping close to the building and away from the streetlights. I had gone to the bottom of the back garden earlier, on the pretence of bringing clothes in from the line, but a pair of pigeons had appeared almost immediately, and I'd had to step back inside. I had no idea if I was being watched. At any rate, Seb hadn't found me yet.

My thoughts drifted to my parents, who weren't really my parents, and home. A wave of emotion rippled through me. What were they thinking? Did they believe that I had disappeared or did they know that Seb was trying to kill me? I had checked the communicator every day, hoping for a message, but there was nothing. And each time I tried to send one, the signal was blocked. Was Rio back from her mission? I wondered. My throat tightened. I wanted to talk to her so badly.

Finally, the clock showed seven thirty. Mrs Duggan swept out, with instructions about leaving lights on for her late return and locking the back door. Her husband barely looked up. He was enveloped in a television programme about people learning to dance. I turned to go upstairs when the doorbell rang.

'I'll get it,' I called.

The social worker. How long would she stay? How could I get rid of her?

I opened the door. The shock all but knocked me over. Seb Roy's dark eyes stared at me. I threw myself against the door in an effort to close it, but he was stronger and shoved me back into the hall. I screamed as my shoulder hit the wall. Seb's hand covered my mouth.

'Don't make a sound,' he said, his lips pressed against my ear. 'I will kill you if I have to. Now quietly walk out that door. If you alert the old man, I will kill him too. It's really all up to you, Aria.'

I could feel something digging into my side. He would kill me, and he would kill Mr Duggan too. I went with him. I imagined Megan waiting for me. What would she think? Would she ever know what really happened?

He had a car outside. He opened the passenger side and pushed me in. The last thing I saw was a pigeon staring at me from a tree in the neighbouring garden. My body had gone into shock. I tried to breathe calmly and escape into a meditative state, but that wasn't easy to do when your body had gone to war. And that was how I felt – as though I were on the highest alert, in a place where everything was in focus with bright, sharp edges.

'Not easy on Earth, is it?' Seb's voice cut through my thoughts.

I didn't answer.

'Not as easy to breathe and withdraw. Earth is more savage, I find. More unpredictable. That said, you are also unpredictable. Did you feel a pull? I could never figure out what you remembered. Your earliest memories, that is. I never knew if you were being honest with me. Were you?'

Again, I didn't answer, but I was processing every word at top speed.

I could never figure out what you remembered.

Did you feel a pull?

A pull towards Earth? Because of my DNA? No, I had not. And I had only been a baby – how could I remember?

He didn't speak after that. I watched the dark night of Dublin pass by, rain and wind, bright, ghostly streetlights, people passing, heads down, fighting the weather. From time to time I stole a glance at his face. My father's face. The face of a monster. How could I be related to him?

The car stopped. We were in some sort of industrial estate. By the distant streetlights I could see the hulking shapes of squat buildings stretching out across the landscape. He got out. My door opened and I got out too. At that moment the moon slid out from behind a cloud and I could read a worn sign on the wall. *Pickering Communication.*

He pushed me ahead of him, swiftly crossing the yard, stopping at a large grey steel door. He pushed his shoulder against it and it fell open. His hand moved and the space was flooded with light. I looked around. An empty space, breeze blocks, cold concrete floor, no heat. Against the far wall there was a table and two chairs. Gusts of cold wind swept through the room from a window-opening with no glass. I shivered. Temperature adjustment was the least of my troubles now.

'Not very comfortable, I'm afraid,' he said. 'But private – and that suits our purposes. I'd rather talk face to face than in the car, wouldn't you? Sit.'

I sat on the chair. He perched on the table looking down at me. I tried to read his eyes. How many times had I looked into them before, as he conducted his tests?

'I know about Kanise.'

The words hovered in the air. Seb looked like I'd just shot him. Even in the midst of all that was happening, I was delighted to knock the smug look off his face.

'How do you …?' he spluttered.

I let him stew for a minute and then I answered him. 'I know everything – or almost everything. You are my father. I am Kanise's child, aren't I?'

'Stop saying her name,' he said, his eyes wild.

I kept my voice low and steady. I was going to finish what I had started. He was going to face what he had done, and I was going to make him do it.

'Why do you hate me?' I asked. 'Why did you always hate me?'

A cloud passed over his face, and for a minute I knew he wasn't there – he was somewhere in his head. Was he back at Kanise's bedside as she lay dying?

'You killed her,' he said, and I could hear the venom in his voice.

I knew that he was barely rational any more, if he ever had been.

'I was a baby,' I said, and despite my best efforts I could feel tears sting my eyes. 'I was a baby. I didn't kill anyone.'

He looked away from me.

'I loved her and you killed her. You killed her. She died trying to deliver you. I wanted nothing more than to get rid of you, but I couldn't …'

'Because you promised her that you'd take care of me. Take me home with you.'

He nodded. 'That was a mistake. Pure sentiment and misplaced loyalty. I took you back and passed you off to your parents as their own. The child they had conceived didn't thrive. I was your physician and I could keep you from being discovered. You are half human, half Terrosian, with some modifications, of course. Well, quite a few modifications actually. You were in line for cystic fibrosis and possibly breast cancer if I hadn't intervened. You were born with red blood like your mother. You can't fool science. The maternal gene was dominant. Your DNA was human and your blood red. I changed the colour of your blood so that you wouldn't be discovered. But you haven't told me how you know all this.'

He hesitated, and I could almost see the pieces falling into place in his brain.

'You found my memory disc!'

I didn't answer.

'I went back and searched for it,' he said. 'I should have realised. Give it to me!'

I didn't care about him or his disc. I knew that I had to stay focused.

'So you took a half-human child back to Terros and kept it secret all these years?'

'Yes,' Seb said, and I could hear something like pride in his voice. 'Yes, I did. I don't know of anyone else who could have pulled it off, but I did.'

Anger boiled inside me, but I pushed it down.

'My parents? What have you done to them?'

'Me? Nothing. They are still under lock and key, lest they try to help you. Heartbroken, of course …'

'You said they didn't want me back.'

'So I did. And did that cause you a lot of pain, Aria?' His eyes mocked me. 'I didn't want you trying to contact them or trying to make your way home. They are heartbroken, but Terros will take care of them. They are prisoners of the state, accused of treason. They were planning to destroy Earth – that is treason.'

'But my dad only did what you instructed him to do. *You* are the traitor, not him!'

Seb shrugged.

'Did they know?' I went on. 'Did they know that I was half human?'

'Of course not! No-one knows and no-one will ever know. If you came back to Terros now, you would be subjected to the most rigorous tests to ensure you weren't carrying the virus. Those tests would show that you are not what you seem, and your ... unusualness would have my fingerprints all over it. I can't let that happen. The next leader of Terros must have an unblemished record. I hope you understand.'

He raised the gun.

Another one, I thought irrelevantly. He seemed to have endless supplies of the most unexpected things.

22

alk, I told myself. *Say something.*

'Kanise would never forgive you.'

'She's dead,' he said, and I saw the emptiness in his eyes. That tactic was not going to work. I tried again. 'You won't get away with this. People on Terros already suspect you.'

He paused. 'No. They don't.'

I started to retreat, stepping backwards, carefully placing my feet, a plan forming in my head. 'They do. My father sent me a message, warning me. He knew you wanted to destroy me.'

Seb frowned. 'That is not true. Your father has no idea. He thinks I am here tracking the virus. Besides, we monitored all his correspondence.'

Another step. It was getting colder. I had to be nearer the window.

'I don't lie. Besides, you can see for yourself. I have the communicator we used in my pocket.'

'Give it to me.'

I took the device from my pocket. He took a step forward. I raised my hand and brought the communicator down hard on his wrist. He screamed. His gun fired with a deafening sound. I threw myself at the open window. My shoulder hit the ground hard but I managed to scramble to my feet.

Run! my brain screamed at me. Another blast from the gun as a bullet whizzed past me. I ran faster, arms pumping. I could hear him behind me. I zig-zagged through the yard, hoping to make myself less of a target. I was calm. All my energy was focused on escaping, but pain was already searing my lungs, hot air burning me with every breath. I gulped the cool night air and kept moving. I felt the lip of a path and stepped up on to it. One more step, faster, head down. Don't look back. But I had to, I had to see what he was doing. He loomed in the darkness. I could make out that he was aiming the gun again, trying to steady his arm without breaking stride.

Crack!

A nugget of asphalt flew up from the yard, hitting my shin, slicing it to the bone. I screamed and fell off the edge of the path. My arms flailed wildly, trying to stop my fall, but it was pointless. The energy of my fall carried me down a rough grassy slope. I was picking up speed, unable to brake, faster and faster, till my feet went from under me altogether, and I fell, striking the ground hard, and then rolling, rolling over stones and thistles and rough grass until my body finally came to rest at the foot of a concrete wall. My hand slapped down on the hard ground and I felt something scratch my skin. I looked down. There was a shard of glass half buried in the ground. With my nails I clawed the soil, releasing it. Glass. And sharp. I picked it up and dropped it into my pocket.

'Aria!'

I looked up and saw him sliding down the hillock towards me. He reached out and grabbed my arm, pulling me to my feet. I cried out, a strangled sob. His fingers dug into my arm.

'Come on!' he said, and I could hear the barely suppressed panic in his voice. He pulled me up the hill.

Why didn't he shoot me? My eyes were growing used to the dark and I realised that the motorway was on the other side of the concrete wall. He couldn't risk someone hearing the shot. He dragged me across the yard, my feet slipping and sliding, the pain in my leg getting worse. We were almost back at the warehouse. I had to do something. I slid my hand into my pocket. Felt the jagged edge of the glass. I grasped it, but my hand was damp with sweat and I almost dropped it. I steadied myself. Felt for it again. I had a comfortable grip now. I had to do this quickly, I told myself. Quickly and decisively. I raised my arm and thrust the shard of glass into the soft flesh of his upper arm.

His scream rent the air. Instinctively, his gun hand went to protect the injury. The gun fell to the ground.

My hand dived for it. My fingers gripped the handle. It felt warm from where he had held it. I straightened my arm, pointing the gun directly at his head. He looked up.

'Move!' I said.

'You've hurt me!' His voice was high and strained.

Blood seeped from the wound on to his hand. I saw the rage in his eyes.

'I'm bleeding,' he said.

I jabbed him with the gun again.

'Move or I will pull the trigger.'

He moved. I got him to the warehouse. Inside, I stood, momentarily uncertain.

'Take out your phone,' I said. 'Lay it on the ground.'

I didn't want to get too close to him. He laid the phone on the floor.

'Kick it over here.'

He did. I picked it up.

'Lie on the floor,' I said. 'Face down.'

He turned his back to me and I relaxed for a moment. He was going to obey me. I almost missed the second in which he turned. Suddenly he lunged, grabbing my gun hand. I tried to push him away, but he was too strong. The gun fell. I could feel his breath on my face. He was wrestling with one hand only, and even so, I couldn't seem to get away from him. In desperation, I kicked out and made contact with his shin. He winced, but didn't slacken his hold. I went for his throat, the palm of my hand pushing his chin up. He faltered. Once more I attacked him, this time aiming for the wound in his upper arm. I felt the edge of the glass protruding from the cut and pushed on it as hard as I could. He screamed and fell back. Moving faster than I ever had before, I dropped to the floor and grabbed the gun again.

I backed out of the room, the gun still trained on him. He knelt on the floor, blood pulsing from his wound. His face was grey with a sheen of sweat and I heard him groan. At the door, I turned and sprinted. This time it was easier. My eyes adjusted to the gloom and I followed the path I had taken earlier, ignoring the pain in my leg, ignoring everything except the way ahead. At the place where I had fallen I stopped and looked back. There was no sign of Seb Roy. I threw the gun into the undergrowth. Then, I took out the phone and rang the number the social worker had given me. It rang four times before she picked up and I wanted to scream with frustration.

'Hello?'

'This is Aria,' I said. The woman tried to interrupt but I continued relentlessly. 'I will only say this once. My father, Seb Roy, is at the old Pickering Communication warehouse. I don't know the address. He is wounded, but he can walk, so the police need to get there quickly.'

Without waiting for a reply, I hit the red button to finish the call.

23

trudged on to the road. My body ached, but surprisingly I felt quite uplifted. I had done something. Despite the craziness of the situation, I had survived. It made me feel good, that little rush of confidence. Things could not have been more out of control, and yet I had survived. *Like humans do*, a small voice said in my head. *Yes*, I thought. *Like humans do*.

I had lost the communicator. There would be no more messages from my father.

I walked bent over against the cold, with no idea where I was going. Cars whizzed by on the motorway, their lights glaring, then vanished, devoured by the night. After some time walking I saw the flashing lights of three police cars, followed by an ambulance. I hoped they'd get there before Seb took off again.

After another half hour of painful walking, I came to a pedestrian bridge that went over the motorway. The wind whipped the hair from my face. People passed by without a glance, huddled against the elements. I descended the bridge and found myself in what appeared to be a residential area.

If I could get to St Brigid's Road, I might at least find Megan, if she had gone back there after I failed to turn up at our meeting point. After that I didn't know what I would do.

I walked in what I hoped was the direction of the city. My mind kept rerunning the conversation I had had with Seb. I was an experiment that went wrong. Funny, I thought I'd been a love-child, but maybe his relationship with Kanise had started out as an experiment?

I tried to do what I had been trained from childhood to do: not to nourish negative thoughts. When I was little, my mother used to say *Spin them, Aria! Spin them!* I tried to spin them now. Put a better face on them. My parents weren't my biological parents, but I loved them and they loved me. I was part-human, but human was not all bad. I was an experiment only in Seb's eyes.

I closed my eyes and took deep breaths, letting the peace I was used to flood my body. It helped. How did I know that what Seb told me was the truth? And yet it felt like the truth. His particular interest in me through the years, the glitches in my immune system, the feeling that I didn't fully belong.

I hurried on. I knew that I had to go back to Rossport and find the star-ship, the one Seb had landed in. I had no proof that it was there, but the logical thing was that all ships would land in the same place. I could only hope I was right.

Then another thought tumbled into my brain. If I were to leave Earth tomorrow, I had to retrieve my bodysuit first. I didn't relish the trip on a dark wet evening. Maybe it could wait until morning?

I had done a bit of walking in circles but I'd found my way by now, and I wasn't far from St Brigid's Road. There was no point in going there. It was too late. Megan would be asleep. I didn't want someone to see me hanging around outside and call the police. I would have to wait until morning to try to meet Megan.

I saw a bridge hunkered over the canal. I'd seen homeless humans sleep in these places before. I went across and tried to block out the smell of urine and rubbish. There was no-one there. I sat down on the cold wet ground and looked at the sky and the pinprick stars. Somewhere out there was my home, my people.

Would I ever see it again? The thought nagged like a dull tooth-ache. I was haunted by the image of my body falling from the sky, leaving my home further and further behind, plummeting towards Earth and a totally different life.

The morning broke slowly and painfully. My whole body hurt and I was hungry and dehydrated.

I needed to see Megan. I pulled myself to my feet.

Some time later I was standing across the road from Megan's apartment block. I looked up to the third floor and saw the warm light through the window. Could I risk going in? Were they still watching the apartment? I hesitated. Why hadn't I taken note of Megan's number? I had only seen it once. The day I was sick. I tried to recall it. I could see the scrap of lined paper. Blue lines on white. I concentrated harder. The numbers started to come into focus. My heart quickened. I pulled out Seb's phone and dialled.

'Hello?'

A man's voice.

'Hello?'

I had to answer.

'I need to talk to Megan,' I said at last.

'Wrong number,' the voice said crisply and then I was listening to the dial tone. Tears filled my eyes. I tried to stay calm. I called up the memory from my mind again. My hand shook as I dialled for the second time.

'Hello?'

Relief spread through me.

'Megan!'

Her voice was little more than a whisper.

'Aria?'

'I'm outside. Please come.'

The line went dead. I waited. Maybe Megan wouldn't come. Maybe she'd decided to have no more to do with me. What did it matter anyway? Practically, Megan could be of little help. And yet, I knew that I needed her.

A few seconds later Megan was hurrying across the road towards me.

'What happened?' Megan's voice had an edge.

'He found me. Seb. He tried ... tried to kill me.'

'What? Are you all right? Where is he now?'

Megan looked around as though expecting him to appear.

'I stabbed him.'

Megan's jaw fell open. 'You did?'

'I did. With a piece of glass.'

'You can't stay here, Aria. The police could come back at any time. They still think you are a terrorist.'

'I've been thinking about the ship. Seb Roy's star-ship. I have to get to Rossport.'

'I'll help you,' Megan said without hesitating.

I looked at her. 'Why?'

'You helped Duke. You didn't have to, but you did.'

'Thank you.'

I felt the weight of sadness lift a little.

'Do you have money?' Megan asked.

'Some.'

'I'll sneak you into our apartment. Mam will have left with Ben by now. You can get something to eat and we can make a plan.'

I followed her without argument across the street and into the building. As soon as we got to the apartment, I went straight to the television to hear the news. I needed to know what had happened to Seb.

I wasn't disappointed. It was the first item on the bulletin.

A man has been arrested ... suspect in terrorist attack ... developed medical complications and is being treated at a local hospital.

I nodded to myself. Medical complications. Bright blue blood for one thing. How would the humans deal with that?

Megan fussed over me, giving me a banana sandwich and hot tea. She wrote a note to her mother, telling her some of what was happening. I explained to her about needing to fetch my bodysuit and Megan planned our trip. All the time I was terrified that the police would show up and that I'd be caught before I got to Rossport.

Twenty minutes later, we hurried out into a cold, wet morning. Shredded grey clouds hung low over the city. I kept my head down to stop the pinpricks of rain from lashing my face. The cold water found its way down the back of my collar and ran in rivulets down my spine. We took a bus, Megan leading the way. The air in the bus was warm from the people who sat hunched in their seats. We found two empty places and sat.

Traffic was heavy and the bus crawled across the city until we got to the left-luggage place in the city centre where Dad and I had left our bodysuits. Megan checked her phone to find out about trains to Rossport, and I went straight to the locker and inputted the code that I had memorised. The door snapped open and there was the suit, still in the bag I had put it in. I felt a pang, a physical pain, when I saw that my father's suit was gone.

There were toilets nearby and I made straight for them. There was no-one there and I opened a cubicle door and went in. I stripped off my human clothes and put on the suit. It felt so good. I realised that I hadn't been complete without it. It was like finding the other part of myself. Instantly, my body was comfortable. A small vibration on my right wrist warned me to drink something: my hydration levels had dropped. That was the least of my problems. I put my human clothes back on over the bodysuit. Then I went back to Megan.

'You got it?' she said.

I nodded.

'Good,' she said. 'I've figured out how to get to Rossport. We need to take a mainline train. We can walk to the station; it's not far.'

I followed her along the wide street. I didn't take much notice of where we were going, but it wasn't long before we arrived at the station. Megan went to buy the tickets. I waited, pacing anxiously, trying to imagine what the next hours would bring.

'The next train leaves from platform two,' Megan said, 'but not for another hour. Let's get a coffee.'

I followed her to a coffee shop and sat and drank the milky liquid. It was pretty horrible, but at least it was warm.

Eventually, the train arrived on the platform. We climbed on and found seats together in the middle of the train. It reminded me of my first trip with my dad on this same train. Tears stung my eyes. Dad. I missed him so badly. I tried not to think about what my parents had been going through. There was no point in looking back: I had to look ahead.

The journey seemed to take for ever. Megan chatted on and off, but I couldn't engage.

'We're slowing down,' Megan said.

'Are we there already?'

'No, that's the thing. This is the express. Why is it stopping?'

We didn't have long to wait for an answer. The voice on the public address system was calm but firm.

'This is an unscheduled stop. Gardaí will now board the train. Please remain seated and await further instructions.'

I felt my heart flutter.

'Are they looking for me?'

Megan shrugged. 'I don't know. Here, put this on.'

She pulled off her black baseball cap and handed it to me. Then she produced a novel from her bag. 'Read this. If they are looking for you, we'll know soon enough, no point making it easy for them.'

I sank back in my seat. There was nothing I could do now. Nothing.

The policemen walked through. Two of them, both young, a metallic sounding voice coming from one of their radios. They looked right and left as they walked, moving quickly along. I held my breath as they passed, but they barely glanced at me.

A man in the seat in front of us stopped them. 'What's all this, then? What's happened?'

'Nothing to worry about, sir. We are looking for a particular gentleman that we believe may be on the train.'

'A criminal?'

The man leant forward and I could see that he was old, his skin wrinkled, a few strands of grey hair on his head.

The policeman nodded. 'That's what we believe.'

He hurried on before the old man could say any more. Relief coursed through me. They weren't looking for me. The danger had passed. Within minutes the train started again.

I glanced at Megan but her eyes were closing. I decided to let her sleep. I had something I needed to do. Carefully I removed the silver disc that I had hidden in my jeans pocket. Seb's memory disc. I had to find where he'd left the star-ship. I slipped the disc into my ear. I tried to call up his last trip. There was nothing. My heart plummeted. I had been stupid to expect to find that information. It was too recent. He would be carrying that memory in his head. But I was able to find a visit he had made in the past. Rossport. He *had* landed in Rossport. And being Seb, he had even remembered the coordinates of the exact location where he had docked his ship. I smiled despite myself.

24

The train trundled on. As we approached our destination, Megan woke up.

'What's the plan now?'

I steadied myself and answered her. 'Find the star-ship and go home. That's the plan.'

Megan smiled wryly. 'All sorted then.'

'Yes.'

'Are you going to be able to drive this space-ship when you get to it?' Megan asked suddenly.

'I hope so,' I said. 'I've been studying the procedures through Seb's ... Seb's memory disc.'

'You have his memory disc?' Megan was looking at me wide-eyed.

'I do. I got it from him when he attacked me in Duke's hideout. To be honest, I'd forgotten about it.'

'And you can figure out how to fly the space-ship from his memories?'

'Yes,' I said. 'He's flown it so many times, all the information is there.'

'What was that like?'

I frowned. 'What?'

'Being in Seb's head.'

I wanted to tell her how horrible it had felt, fumbling through his memories, feeling what he felt, but I couldn't. There were no words.

'It was a means to an end,' I said.

Megan looked through the window. The day was overcast and the sky heavy with rain. When she turned to me, her eyes were wide and unfocused.

'Will I ever see you again?'

I could hear the loneliness in her voice and I felt a pinch in my heart. I hadn't thought about that.

'I don't think so,' I said. 'But I hope I can persuade my people to stop using you as a Shadow Planet. They need to understand that you do have feelings. That you do form relationships.'

'Do you think that will make a difference?'

I closed my eyes for a second. Would it make a difference? In my heart I believed it would. Not to someone like Seb, but to my parents and people like them. It wouldn't be easy, but they would care.

I turned to Megan. 'I think it will make a difference. Yes.'

'I can't believe I've met an alien,' Megan said. 'And you haven't really told me much about your planet. Do you miss it?'

'Very much,' I said, and let my mind drift for a second back to Terros. I could almost smell the fragrant air, feel the soft breeze on my cheeks.

'And Earth?' Megan looked at me quizzically. 'What do you think about Earth?'

For a second I considered telling her the full truth. What would Megan think if she knew that I was half human? But just as quickly, I decided against it. I wasn't human in any real sense. My home was on Terros. Telling Megan the whole story would only confuse things. I focused on Megan's question. What *did* I think about Earth? I remembered that moment in the star-ship when Dad had shown me the flashing beacon that led us in. My heart almost stopped. The beacon! Why hadn't I thought of it before? I could make sure my people never came to Earth ever again. Excitement coursed through me. If they couldn't find Earth, they couldn't interfere with Earth or harm it, now or in the future.

'Aria!' Megan was looking at me, puzzled. 'What's wrong? Why are you looking at me like that?'

'Sorry!' I said. 'I was thinking about something else. You asked me about Earth?'

'Yes,' she said. 'What do you feel about it now?'

'I never thought I would like it here,' I said finally. 'It is so wild, so uncertain, but I do. I do like it and I know that it's wrong what Terros is doing. You have the right to be free, we all do.'

Before I could say any more, Megan nudged me. 'I think we're here,' she said.

We started to collect our belongings. It was as we left the station that I saw him, or thought I did. A man ducked past the men's toilets, shoulders hunched, eyes on the floor. I stopped dead.

'What is it?'

I could hear Megan's voice but I was frozen in that moment. *Seb.* He was here.

'Aria?'

'I'm sorry ... I think ... I just saw Seb.'

'Here? How could you? He's been arrested. You said so yourself.'

'I know, but I saw him. Over there.'

Megan looked back in the direction I had been staring in. There was no-one to be seen.

'It's your imagination. Come on! Let's get to the ship.'

'I can't go there until it's dark. Don't want to be seen.'

'Come on! We'll get you something to eat before you have to head off.'

178

Megan strode out of the station. I followed her, stopping every few seconds to look back. There was no sign of Seb. Maybe I *had* imagined it. But I couldn't think about that now. I had to concentrate.

The small village was quiet, with only the odd person hurrying by, collar pulled up against the wind and drizzling rain.

'Look!' Megan said. 'That pub is open and they serve food. We missed lunch. Come on!'

When we got to the pub, the door was ajar. I could hear music as we pushed our way through. Inside, the room was low-ceilinged, with a bar tucked away in the corner. Beyond that was a low arch leading into a bigger room full of tables and chairs. At one table a group of musicians sat playing.

'Well, girls?' A woman addressed us from behind the bar. She was tall and skinny with neat features and bright eyes that looked us up and down with a naked curiosity. Before I could react, Megan stepped forward.

'We're just waiting for my parents. They told us to come here and get something to eat. They'll be along shortly. They got caught in the rain.'

'In you go, then,' the woman said. 'I'll bring you menus. Four of you, you say?'

'Yes.' Megan nodded.

The woman looked at me. 'Where are you from, then? Not around here, I'd say,' she said.

'London,' I answered, without hesitation.

Megan jumped in. 'Me too. We're all here together for a break.'

The woman nodded. 'Follow me.'

She led us to a table near where the musicians sat. I glanced over at them. They had stopped playing and were laughing loudly at something the man at the centre had said.

'That's Máirtín O'Donnell,' the woman hissed, nodding furtively at the musicians. 'The accordion player. Do ye know him? He's famous.'

I shook my head.

'No,' I said. 'I don't think so.'

The woman nodded, handing over two menus. 'He's from Galway.'

'We're from London,' I said.

'Ah, well,' the woman said. 'He's a good accordion player. They're practising for a concert tonight.'

The woman hurried away. Megan smiled.

'What?' I said.

'Maybe let me do the talking,' Megan said. 'I'll go up and order. What would you like?'

I chose the vegetarian dish of the day and Megan went to the bar. We ate our meal and chatted. I felt like I had known Megan for a long time. She was good company – clever, like Rio, and funny too.

After a while, the bar woman brought us a deck of cards.

'Here, these might keep you amused for a while,' she said kindly. 'Looks like your parents have been delayed.'

Megan nodded. 'Thanks.'

She taught me how to play poker, and we whiled away the time as the light outside faded and lights were turned on in the pub. I knew that it was nearly time to go, but Megan seemed intent on prolonging the departure.

'They have really good chocolate cake,' she said to me when we had grown tired of the card game. 'I'll go up and get some.'

'I really need to go soon, Megan,' I said gently.

'I know,' she said. 'But a slice of cake won't kill you.'

Before I could object, she was up at the counter ordering coffee and cake. I shrugged. Another few minutes wouldn't hurt.

Megan was on her way back to the table when someone switched on the television. I stared at the screen.

'What is it?' Megan said.

'Look!'

It was Seb. I felt the world slip away from me.

Suspected terrorist has escaped police custody today as he was being moved across country. Police have issued a warning that he is violent and extremely dangerous …

'It *was* him,' I said. 'It was him at the station.'

'What'll we do?' Megan was already on her feet.

I tried to think. He had come here for the same reason I had, and he too would be waiting for darkness to fall. But where was he now?

'We should call the guards. We could say we've seen him.'

'Good thinking,' I said. 'If they get here in time.'

Megan picked up her phone and dialled.

'No good,' she said. 'No signal.'

'Try outside,' a man's voice said.

It was the accordion player. 'There's better signal there at the back door.'

'I'll go,' Megan said. 'You stay here.'

The musician walked back to his seat. The music started again. I tried to relax but my whole body felt tense. Where was Seb now? What would he do if he found me here in this pub? It was only when the music stopped and the musicians went to the bar that I realised that Megan hadn't come back.

Panic tightened my throat. Where was she? I could hear the thud, thud of my heart, battering against my ribs. I got up and headed for the door.

Outside, the darkness had fallen, covering everything in murky black. I could hear the sea, and the wind tore at my hair. Outside the door was a deck with wooden steps leading to the beach below. I scanned the beach. Nothing. I ran down the steps holding on to the smooth wooden banister rail. My feet sank into the soft sand.

'Megan!'

My voice sounded strained to my own ears. I took a deep breath and tried again.

'Megan!'

Nothing. Only the sound of the waves breaking on the shore and the mewling wind. Where was she? I turned to go back up the steps and saw him in the light from the pub. Under the wooden stairs, he stood holding Megan in front of him, his hand clamped on her mouth, his teeth white in the dim light.

'Let her go,' I said. 'You want me. Let her go.'

'I'll let her go when you give me back my memory disc.'

I said nothing, but my thoughts were flying as he spoke. I had a bargaining chip. Something he wanted. That was more than I could have hoped for. I couldn't mess this up. If I did, he could kill Megan. I knew what he was capable of.

'Hand it over and I will let her go.'

'No,' I said. 'It's worth more than that to you. You let us both go and you never come back here. You go home and tell them that Earth isn't safe any more.'

Seb frowned.

'You leave me here on the Shadow Planet. You don't need to kill me. Kill the pigeons, persuade our people that Earth isn't safe, and they'll never come back here. That way, they will never learn what you did. No-one will ever see me again. Your secret would be safe.'

Megan struggled, trying to break away, but Seb yanked her back.

'Aria,' she shouted. 'Don't do this. You'll never get home.'

'All right,' Seb cut across her. 'Give me my disc and I'll leave. I could kill you both, but that news might reach Terros. You stay here and die here. When I am leader, I will persuade Terros that we can't come back to Earth ever again. Now hand over the disc.'

It was only then that the reality of the situation dawned on me. I would never see Terros again. Never see my parents. Seb would take the star-ship, the only way back. And he would lead Terros into the future. Tears welled in my eyes, but I had made my mind up. There was no alternative. This was the way it would have to be. I couldn't live with myself if he hurt Megan. I took the disc from my pocket and started to walk towards him.

'Don't do it,' Megan said, but I wasn't listening.

I took another step and everything happened at once. Blue lights flashed in my face. A voice rang out from the steps above us through a megaphone.

'Put down your weapon. This is the Garda Síochána. You are surrounded.'

Seb, distracted, let Megan go. She threw herself on the sand. I dashed for the stairs. Out of the corner of my eye I saw Seb turn and start to run towards the sea. A shot rang out. For a second, it seemed that the Earth stopped spinning. In slow motion, I watched Seb stumble and then fall. Within seconds, men in uniform surrounded him. Megan must have got through to the police before Seb got hold of her.

Megan clutched my arm.

'Go, Aria! Go before the guards see you.'

We stood facing one another, and my heart felt almost too full to speak, but I tried.

'Thank you for everything,' I said.

'I won't ever forget you,' Megan replied.

'I won't forget you either,' I said, 'and I won't forget Ed Sheeran or Ben or Duke,' I added, trying not to cry. 'I'll do everything I can to save your planet. I promise you that.'

'I know you will,' Megan said. 'Just remember to keep on dancing.'

I pulled her into a quick hug and saw the tears standing in her eyes and felt my own tears on my cheeks.

I pulled away then and ran to the water, shedding the human clothes as I went, until finally there was only my bodysuit covering me. With a final look back, I walked into the tide.

HOW IT ENDED

I slipped into the driving pod of the star-ship *Somnius*, Seb's ship. I quietened my mind, pushing away the frantic images of the last few hours. The suit regulated my temperature; I felt my heart slow down and my thoughts quietened. I drew up from my short-term memory all that I'd learnt from Seb's memory disc.

Within seconds, the ship had moved out of the ocean and back up into the atmosphere. Once it broke through Earth's stratosphere, the *Somnius* slowed. I looked out through the porthole and saw the Shadow Planet, azure blue and white, a small miracle shining out of the surrounding darkness. It was just as beautiful now as that first time I'd seen it and this time I wasn't falling. This time, I felt like I belonged, with one home above me and another below. And then I saw the pulsing light flashing on the Icarus Wall just like I had seen it on the day I arrived with Dad. The beacon! Using every atom of concentration that I possessed, I zoomed in on it, and pinpointed its location exactly. Immediately, data appeared on the screen showing its longitude and latitude. Then another menu appeared, giving me all of my options.

All I saw was the word DESTROY.

I only hesitated for a second, and the thought that held me back was a selfish one. If I chose that option, I could never return. Humans would be free to live their lives as they pleased. My people would never be able to find Earth again and wouldn't be able to deliver the killer dose of the virus. Megan and Ben and Duke and

Grace and all the people that I had met would be safe. Their lives would go on, and they would evolve in their own time, in their own way. Apart from Megan, they would never know the part that we had played in their history, or even that Terros existed. And they would never know that I had come here for a short time and made a difference.

A pang of loneliness hit me that I didn't expect, followed by something deeper. I was about to cut all links with a part of myself, and it hurt – but not enough to stop me. With a steady hand, I selected DESTROY, and in one heartbeat, the beacon disappeared, leaving only darkness.

I sat for a minute looking at the black screen; then I turned the ship away from the blue planet. I turned and headed for home.

ACKNOWLEDGEMENTS

My agent, Anne Clark, is everything one could ask for in an agent and I am forever in her debt for her insightful suggestions and never-ending support.

The team at Little Island have been a pleasure to work with in the making of this book. Thank you to Matthew Parkinson-Bennett, Kate McNamara and Elizabeth Goldrick for all your care and expertise in bringing this book into the world. Special thanks to Siobhán Parkinson, my editor, who was as creative and patient as she always is, and now knows far more about pigeons than she ever intended.

Copy-editor Emma Dunne did a wonderful and thorough job and made me look a lot smarter than I am. I love the cover art for this book and all credit to Jeff Langevin for that.

I get tremendous support from all my friends, whose names I cannot mention lest I forget one. These are the people whose eyes glaze over when you tell them about the latest plot twist, but carry on regardless, and put the kettle on for more tea.

Lots of young people read my previous books and made me welcome in their schools. I am very grateful to them all. I still have no power to give you a homework pass, but I am working on it. Keep the faith.

Children's Books Ireland are a wonderful resource for any writer. They provide us with *Inis Magazine*, uplifting coffee mornings, and wonderful conferences, along with advice and encouragement. Sincere thanks to them for all that they do.

I received a literature bursary from the Arts Council of Ireland while I was working on this novel. It came at a crucial time and gave me the encouragement to finish what I had started. I am very grateful.

Thank you to all my writer and illustrator friends, especially the Wonderfest gang, who got me through Covid and beyond. They are an inspiration.

My family – mother, sisters, nieces and nephews – are the best. I am very fortunate to have them. My brother-in-law, Brian Miles, was unofficial researcher of all things wildlife for this book – I am delighted that my sister married him.

Finally, the people who live with me – my husband, Padraic, and my son and daughter, James and Rosa, are there for all the ups and downs. I love you all.

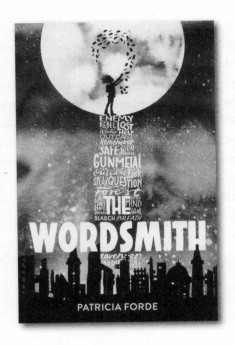

How many words do you need to survive?

'Love', 'hope', 'freedom' – in the dystopian
future of Ark, after climate change disaster, these words are
being banned. One girl takes a stand against this
loss of language – she is the Wordsmith.

Winner of a White Raven Award from the International Youth Library
A Library Association of America Notable Book for Children
Over 60,000 copies sold worldwide

Published in the USA as *The List*

ABOUT PATRICIA FORDE

PATRICIA FORDE lives in Galway, in the west of Ireland. She has published many books for children, in Irish and English, as well as plays, soap operas and television drama series. In another life, she was a primary school teacher and the artistic director of Galway Arts Festival. Two of her novels with Little Island, *Bumpfizzle the Best on Planet Earth* and *The Wordsmith*, a Library Association of America Notable Book for Children (published in the USA by SourceBooks as *The List*), were awarded White Raven awards by the International Youth Library. Her picturebook *To the Island* was co-published by Little Island and Galway 2020 European City of Culture.

ABOUT LITTLE ISLAND

Little Island is an independent Irish publisher of the best new writing for young readers, founded in 2010 by Ireland's first children's laureate, Siobhán Parkinson. Little Island books are found throughout Ireland, the UK and North America, and have been translated into many languages around the world.

RECENT AWARDS FOR LITTLE ISLAND BOOKS

Spark! School Book Awards 2022: Fiction ages 9+
Wolfstongue by Sam Thompson

Book of the Year
KPMG Children's Books Ireland Awards 2021
Savage Her Reply by Deirdre Sullivan

YA Book of the Year
Literacy Association of Ireland Awards 2021
Savage Her Reply by Deirdre Sullivan

YA Book of the Year
An Post Irish Book Awards 2020
Savage Her Reply by Deirdre Sullivan

White Raven Award 2021
The Gone Book by Helena Close

Judges' Special Prize
KPMG Children's Books Ireland Awards 2020
The Deepest Breath by Meg Grehan

Little Island
Books create waves